TALES OF THE SEA
A SHORT STORY ANTHOLOGY

SUZANNE BAGINSKIE   LINDA M. CRATE

ELAINE DONADIO   R. J. ERBACHER   SHARI HELD

DAVID LANGE   PAUL MILA   MICHAEL O'KEEFE

WILLIAM JOHN ROSTRON   JASMINE TRITTEN

JIM TRITTEN

Tales of the Sea—A Short Story Anthology

Copyright © 2022 by JK Larkin

All rights reserved

Published by Red Penguin Books

Bellerose Village, New York

Library of Congress Control Number: 2022916009

ISBN

Print 978-1-63777-302-4

Digital 978-1-63777-303-1

CONTENTS

A FOREVER LOVE

LINDA M. CRATE

His mother had confessed that his father had been a human, but she warned him not to explore the world above for humans were the most peculiar creatures. Some were honest about their monstrosity and destroyed nature and all of its beautiful creatures without a second thought, some were only monsters to one another, and some were mixed bags of monstrosity. She said some were kind, but it was hard to tell through all the masks and lies they sometimes wove to tell the difference. Even good men told lies, she warned, and so it was best not to be confused and ensnared with the fickle hearts of mankind.

Yet Manavi also told her son Lundetto that he was his destiny was his own to make. She warned him, however, that should he choose to leave the kingdoms of the seas for a land and realm he had never known that he could be utterly changed in ways that he didn't like.

Lundetto didn't have any interest, however, remaining comfortable in the realms of all he had ever known for whilst merpeople varied from ocean to ocean they were all pretty much the same. They may have different customs, different shapes of fins, and different cuisine or music yet they all had the sea in common.

Most seemed to have his mother's opinion of humans, too, and were quite dismissive when he tried to press them for any information he might know about humans.

One merwoman even insisted that humans killed sharks and whales and polluted the sea so she didn't really think there was one really worth knowing.

Surely, she couldn't be right.

The sea gulls he had spoken to, however, had told him much the same. It frustrated him. How could these creatures with legs instead of fins be such wicked beasts?

"They kill crabs, they kill birds, they chop down the very trees that give them the oxygen they breathe!"

Lundetto's long cyan hair fell in a torrent of curls half-way down his back as he broke the surface of the waters. He had observed many ships and many peoples and some seemed to be kind as the soft petal of roses that the dead ones dropped from their hands as they fell into the water. He didn't know the name of the bones in their bodies but he was always curious and examined skeletons. Some were large, some were small, and of course the males varied from the females. They seemed just as vastly different as mermaids could be from one another yet similar. It intrigued him. His cyan eyes gazed upon a ship. There stood a man and a woman laughing together. He watched them. She wore a blue dress and hung dangerously close to the outside of the ship.

"You'll fall off!" her lover warned her.

"No, I won't. Even if I do, I can swim."

"Well, I can't. I don't want anything to happen to you."

So some humans chose to swim and some didn't? Well, that was curious. He wondered why that human man wouldn't decide to swim. Perhaps, he had a fear of water. Just as some merpeople seemed to have a fear of ships and land.

She had dark skin and long curly dark hair and black eyes.

His skin was dark, too, but a lighter shade than hers. His eyes were green and his hair was long and black.

Lundetto put a hand to his pale cheek. His mother said that he had inherited his white skin from his father, but to him it looked more a peach color. He wondered why they called it white. Pale was more accurate.

He swam closer and closer until the boat was within arm's length. He heard the laughter of a second woman. She closely resembled the other girl but her eyes were brown and she was in a pink dress that reminded him of his mother's favorite corals beneath the sea.

"I wonder what it would be like to be kissed by a mermaid."

Oh, now come how he was he supposed to resist that?! He thought, grinning. He climbed up the side of the boat, pulling the girl into a kiss. He then winked, leaping back into the water.

"HE KISSED ME! DID YOU SEE THAT MERMAN KISS ME?!"

"Cheeky bastard!" the other girl shouted.

"I know! I said I wanted a mermaid not a merman!"

Lundetto cocked his head to the side, chuckling. "My bad," he muttered to himself, swimming away, so far down they couldn't possibly find him.

His mother and his older sister Florencia were waiting for him. Neither seemed particularly pleased as if they already knew what had happened.

"Florencia, I met a human who wanted to be kissed by a mermaid today. She wasn't pleased when I kissed her. So there is a chance you can find love, after all," he winked.

"Lundetto! How many times will you go to the surface?! You could be killed," his mother protested.

"You also told me my fate was my own to decide. Come now, mother, aren't you ever curious about humans?"

"You see where my curiosity with humans got me. After Florencia's father died, I fell in love with a human who left when he found out about you. He sneered at me, 'What are you going to leave your precious ocean for me?' Of course, I couldn't do that and he knew it. Some of them are impossibly evil creatures, Lundetto."

"And some of them are kind, too."

"Mother, maybe I should go with him next time to supervise."

"Would you want to do that, Florencia?"

"I'll make sure he won't get in trouble if it would bring you any peace."

"Very well," Manavi nodded.

Florencia had the same dark skin that their mother had, the same amethyst eyes, the same dark plum fins and long flowing plum hair. His mother had said he had gotten his cyan eyes, hair, and fin from his long deceased grandfather. "Why do you have to vex our poor mother so?"

"I don't worry her on purpose, but curiosity isn't something evil or wrong, Florencia. You can't tell me you've never wanted to know about humans. Yes, one burned mother...but they're not all fire. Some of them are just like you and me. The girl wasn't angry I kissed her, she was just angry I was a merman. Maybe you should kiss her tomorrow!"

"I most certainly won't."

"If you did then she could tell us who was the better kisser," he winked.

"Well," Florencia remarked. "Maybe I will then just to put you to shame, brother mine."

When Lundetto woke up the next morning he swished his tail out and swam circles around Florencia.

"We're never going to find that boat, Lundetto."

"Their boats don't go that fast," he insisted. "I remember what the boat looked like. We can find it again. I found it close to the landing near the beach yesterday so they're probably visiting the beach there before continuing onward."

After a few hours of swimming Lundetto spotted the boat that had been drifting slowly through the ocean the day previous. He nodded to himself and he swam over.

"Cora, can you believe it...we're finally here."

The girl who had been clinging so close to the boat's edge the day before looked quite sea sick. "Thank goodness we're visiting the beach today."

"Neve, look at your girlfriend! She looks pathetic."

"Fidelia, come now, be kind to Cora. She's your sister."

"Florencia and Fidelia sound nice together, don't they?" Lundetto winked.

"Be quiet," Florencia hissed, sending him a dark look.

"Oh, look, it's that horrible merman from yesterday!"

"I've brought my sister with me today," Lundetto winked.

Florencia saw the girl glance at her curiously.

"Purple is such a pretty color. It's almost prettier than pink," the girl remarked. Today her dress was a different shade of pink this shade closer to that of what he had seen of roses.

"Florencia likes girls, too," Lundetto winked.

"Lundetto, you jerk, be quiet!"

"Lundetto, eh? That seems the perfect name for a jerk," Fidelia remarked. "Florencia is a pretty name, though."

Fidelia glanced at the merfolk. "What do you two want?"

"Well, since you like girls I thought you could tell us which was the better kisser, myself or my sister."

"I guess since you're here, why not?"

Florencia looked irritated at how quickly Lundetto had revealed the threading of things. She swam over, however, pushing him out of the way as the humans were walking down a long piece of wood that led to land. Florencia climbed to the point where Fidelia was and kissed the young woman square on the mouth. He had expected a quick peck, but both of them seemed interested in more than that.

Lundetto chuckled, splashing them both with water. "You're welcome, lovebirds," he chirped.

"Lundetto, stop!"

"Shall I tell mother the wedding plans?" he winked.

"It's much too soon for that, we've only just met."

"Yet you're kissing like you've known one another for centuries," Lundetto grinned, winking again.

He tried not to get too broody watching as his sister and the girl Fidelia grew closer to one another. He knew it was his fault for introducing them. He did think Florencia deserved to find love, but he wanted to find love, too. One was truly a lonely number. Two could be as well if spent with the wrong person, but he wanted to find the right one.

Lundetto had always liked both men and women. That's just the way he was. This was generally more acceptable in the merfolk population than it was with all the humans he had observed which was why he was pleasantly surprised when he had found someone who could have the capacity of liking his sister.

He wasn't wrong. The relationship between the pair went swimmingly and only seemed to grow stronger with each passing day.

A year later he tried not to be jealous when Florencia married the girl who traded her legs for fins. Yet he couldn't deny how lonely he sometimes got. He wondered if he wasn't just going to have to drag someone human down into the sea so that the wouldn't get lonely.

Ironically as this thought passed the merman's mind Lundetto saw a human fall beneath the waves. Catching the young man in his arms he swam and swam looking for the boat. Unfortunately, the turbulent sea was too ferocious and the boat crashed into ruin. Then Lundetto swam the man to the nearest beach he could find and he knew enough to know that he had to resuscitate him and did so. As the man started coughing up sea water, Lundetto went to swim back to the sea, but the man grabbed his arm.

Lundetto blinked.

"You saved my life. I must thank you somehow."

"A thank you would suffice," the merman remarked, inclining his head.

"Please, my wife and my sister would love to meet you. They always speak of the sea as if she's a person. I would love for them to meet you."

"Okay," Lundetto reluctantly agreed.

Lundetto learned the man's name was Renaldo and his sister's name was Raine. His wife was named Moon like the orb hung in the sky which amused Lundetto some as it seemed a strange name. Though, perhaps, he ought not have laughed because his name seemed strange to most people.

Renaldo had shoulder length black hair, naturally tan skin, and bright brown eyes. Raine had long black hair that fell to her waist in a torrent of black curls, the same naturally dark skin, but her eyes were a blue found neither in the sky nor the sea. They were pale and bright all at once.

Moon was aptly named for, though, despite her youth she had long silver hair and lavender eyes.

For the next year Lundetto got to know both Raine and Moon, but it was Moon that he loved and Moon that loved him.

"But I cannot do this to Renaldo. He is my friend," Lundetto protested.

"My heart cannot live a lie," Moon protested. "We didn't mean for this to happen, it just did."

"It is a betrayal none-the-less," Lundetto insisted. "I cannot do this to, Renaldo."

Raine, having heard them by mistake, stepped forward. "Go, both of you. I will say something terrible happened to Moon and Lundetto overcome with guilt vowed never to return here."

"That's not something I could ask of you," Lundetto protested.

"You didn't," Raine remarked. "I love you, Lundetto, and if she makes you happier than I could then I will let love find it's mark. It cannot be wrong if you found one another, right? Now go before I change my mind."

Moon frowned. "There is one problem, I am not going to be going with him into the sea."

Raine smiled. "I spent a fortune on this. It changes the drinker into a mermaid. I got it from a shop when we were visiting the cave of the four witches."

"You would do this for me? You've always dreamed of the sea, Raine."

"I know, you need not remind me. Go!"

Moon drank the potion, and suddenly her legs were fused together in a fin as lavender as her eyes. She looked into the tear stricken eyes of Raine. "Thank you," she remarked.

Clinging to one another, Moon and Lundetto swam into the sea.

"Are you sure this is what you wanted?"

"Sometimes your heart is wrong. Sometimes you marry the wrong person first, and find your true love second. I couldn't lie to myself anymore, and I know you feel the same way."

Lundetto nodded. He would forever feel guilty not only for hurting Renaldo but Raine. "We will pay for our sins one day."

"It's not a sin to love."

"Do you really not feel guilty?"

"No, because life gave me someone to believe in. Renaldo isn't pure as the driven white snow. You never hurt me as he did. The future is a blank slate and it is ours."

"It is ours," Lundetto agreed. "Are you ready to meet my mother, sister, and sister-in-law?" he asked.

"Aye," Moon smiled.

Lundetto knew that he may always carry uneasiness about him in regards to the situation, but as long as he had Moon by his side he knew that he would be okay. He just hoped that Raine would find someone who deserved her, and that Renaldo would recover. He felt as if love could be a two-edged sword. One that brought with it both happiness and pain. Turning to Moon, though, he could feel nothing but the warmth of her skin. As his lips connected with hers, he knew her words were right. This was true.

Moon was his wish, his dream, his hope. She was a prophecy fulfilled.

He had finally found someone whose wildness played well with his own. Lundetto smiled at Moon. "I love you."

"And I, you," she smiled. "Forever," she vowed.

"Forever," Lundetto nodded.

THE LITTLE MERMAID & THE KRAKEN

SHARI HELD

The Little Mermaid leapt into the waters of the Øresund, which connects the North Sea with the Baltic Sea, taking care to hug the shore. Weeks earlier, she'd plunged deep into the sea, headed for her father's palace, when she realized she could no longer breathe underwater. She'd barely made it back to shore. Now she knew the panic humans experienced when the cold dark waters closed in on them and snuffed out their lives. She didn't want to repeat that near disaster.

Her iridescent tail flipped and waved, as she relished the sensation of refreshing seawater running down her body. All too soon, she would have to return to the shelter of the rocky shore she now called home.

Life had dealt her one cruel blow after another, all because she'd fallen in love with a human prince. She'd even considered ending it all. Letting her beloved sea take her. Instead, she was attempting to come to terms with her limitations.

Hope was a serendipitous commodity to cling to in the bleak, harsh lands and seas once ruled by the fierce Vikings and their Norse gods. According to Nordic legend, the oceans were filled with Kraken and other sea monsters, sea witches, merfolk, and many long-forgotten creatures. King Njor, the god of the wind, sea, and wealth, presided over all. Though the Vikings were long gone, thousands of people still believed in the legends of the sea monsters and the Norse gods. So did she. After all, she'd met some of them herself since becoming landbound.

Once on shore, she fell asleep basking in the sun and did not awaken until the stars shone bright in the inky sky. Then she began to sing so beautifully the wind ceased to blow so her voice could be heard far and wide.

Nearby, in the dark waters a young Kraken named Rungnir drew near. He'd roamed the high seas alone for centuries. Krakens aren't immortal, but when fully grown, they can reach the size of a small island, so no sea creatures can hurt them. Not the great white whale nor the Krakens' much smaller cousins, the Giant Pacific Octopus and the Giant Squid. Only time could sound the death knell for a Kraken.

Sometimes Rungnir, too, felt it would be easier to cease to exist. Humans and sea creatures alike considered him loathsome and feared him. He longed for a friend. Someone to joke with, to raise his spirits when he was down, to share a joyful moment. He hadn't felt like that since his mother died. She'd told him tales of giant sea serpents, gentle merfolk, and his kin—Kraken who lived at the opposite end of the Earth. He thought about trying to find them but hesitated to venture far from the Nordic seas. Truthfully, he wasn't the bravest of Krakens.

During the darkness of night, when the coast was fogged in and the fishing ships safely docked in the harbor, Rungnir emerged and swam as near to shore as he dared, attracted by the twinkling lights, blaring horns, and exotic aromas emanating from land. He pretended the horns were talking to him. Sometimes he even answered back.

One bright moonlit night while floating in the shadows of The Sound, he heard hauntingly beautiful music coming from a rock formation near the shore. Notes sweet and heart-piercingly sad. They resonated with what he felt inside. Rungnir knew he shouldn't swim closer, but the voice mesmerized him.

He slowly emerged to catch a glimpse of the singer of such

touching melodies. A comely young woman with flowing, blonde tresses that caressed her shapely body sat on the rock surrounded by lanterns. She glowed with a soft yellow light.

Is this a mermaid? Rungnir had never seen one, but he'd heard tales about merfolk. His large, round, orange eyes closely scrutinized her. She was so tiny she'd fit inside one of his pockets with room to spare. Yes, that was definitely a mertail folded beneath her. He was so excited he clapped with joy. His arms created a huge wave that crashed onto the shore, soaking her. The mermaid stopped singing, her sea-blue eyes opened wide, and she gazed upon the waters, trying to pierce the darkness. When she spied Rungnir, she shrank back, her face fearful.

"Don't be afraid, young mermaid. I mean you no harm."

"But you are a Kraken, are you not?" She slid behind a rock and cautiously poked her head out to look at him. "Krakens eat merfolk for a snack."

Rungnir moved sideways until she was back in his line of sight. "Have you ever known any merfolk who were eaten or harmed in any way by a Kraken?"

"No, but folklore says you are a wicked, vicious killer of all life you encounter—including merfolk. And that you pluck ships from the sea and swallow them whole, along with all onboard."

"Folklore also says mermaids bewitch sailors with their hypnotic singing causing their ships to crash upon the rocks."

The mermaid drew her torso up straight and glared at him. "That's not true. That's our cousins, the Sirens."

"Well, it's not true that Krakens wreck ships and eat everyone onboard, either." He tilted his head to one side. "Although, a large Kraken, while emerging or submerging from the ocean, could cause a big enough disturbance to capsize a ship. But it wouldn't be intentional."

"I see." The mermaid relaxed her shoulders but didn't budge from the safety of the rock.

"Okay, then. I think we've established that folklore mustn't always be taken at face value. I want to live peacefully with all animals, merfolk, and humans."

A tear slid down Rungnir's face and plopped into the sea. "I'm all alone, now, you see. One day my mother and I were relaxing in the hot August sun, drifting slowly in the calm, warm waters of the Norwegian Sea. She was ancient and fell asleep. I rarely left her side, but that day I forged ahead, attracted by a colorful school of fish I'd never before seen." He wiped the tears from his eyes. "When I returned, I saw the life spirit had left her. I was helpless to do anything but watch as she sank to the bottom of the sea."

The mermaid came out of hiding and scooted closer to Rungnir. "That's such a sad tale. You must be very lonely. I'm so sorry about your mother. I, too, know what it's like to feel all alone."

All three of Rungnir's hearts did a flip-flop. Finally. Someone who understood. "My name's Rungnir. What's yours?"

"They call me The Little Mermaid."

"Hmm. That's not a proper name, is it? Although it is descriptive."

She lowered her eyes and bit her lower lip. "But I'm not a true mermaid. Not anymore."

"Oh?"

"It's a long story."

Rungnir drew closer. "I've nowhere to go."

The Little Mermaid set her lantern close to the edge of the shore. "Once upon a time, I was carefree, happily playing games with my sisters in our underwater kingdom. Then, one spring day, I rescued a handsome, shipwrecked Nordic prince and fell in love with him. It was as if I were enchanted. I couldn't eat. I couldn't sleep. All I wanted to do was swim close to shore and watch and wait until he appeared."

"You had it bad, huh?"

She nodded. "I even beseeched an ancient sea witch to transform me into a human so I could be with him."

Rungnir glanced at her mertail and raised his eyebrows. "How'd that work out?"

"I didn't realize she despised me. She was jealous of my singing voice."

"And what a beautiful voice it is. Your singing is what attracted me to the shore."

The Little Mermaid blushed, then continued. "The witch desired the prince for her own. Her jealousy turned to fury when he vowed to marry the person who had rescued him. Me."

"So she turned you down flat, did she?"

"No. She agreed to create a potion for me *if* I accepted her conditions. One, she would give me human legs, but every step I took would feel as if I were walking on knife points. Two, if the prince married someone other than me, I would turn into seafoam and die the day after the wedding. Finally, she demanded my voice as payment. I was so thoroughly besotted, I agreed."

The Little Mermaid shook her head as if she couldn't believe her own stupidity. "She touched her wand to my tongue, and I was mute. She cackled as she did it, her face so close I could smell her foul, dead breath."

"Are you serious? I think that's against the law. But your prince must have asked you to marry him. You're still alive."

She trembled, whether in anger or fear, Rungnir didn't know and didn't ask.

The Little Mermaid bowed her head and emitted a strangled sob. "I rushed to the prince's side as soon as I was human, but a nobleman's daughter had already proclaimed *she* had saved him. I was mute and couldn't tell him otherwise. Right in front of me, as if I weren't even there, they set the wedding for three months from that day. I poured my grief out to my mermaid sisters, who occasionally swam near the shore to see me. I entreated them to beg the malevolent old witch to give my voice back so I could tell the prince the truth and he would marry me."

"Well, she must have had pity on you because your singing voice is extraordinary."

The Little Mermaid smiled and paused for a breath of air, then continued. "That spiteful old witch has a piece of coal in lieu of a heart. She refused." She bowed her head. "I didn't care if I lived or died."

Rungnir blinked his saucer-like eyes. "I know that feeling."

"But I didn't wallow long in my misery. I applied for a job at the castle. One day, Astrid, a young woman at court, and I were picking chamomile for the kitchen. As we gathered herbs, I replayed the whole sad story in my mind. Turns out Astrid is a witch skilled in telepathy. She told her father, the strongest wizard in all of Scandinavia, about my plight. He intervened and convinced the witch to return my voice. But I had to agree to yet another condition."

"As if she hadn't already asked so much of you. What, this time?"

"I had to retrieve a white feather from the eagle that sits atop Yggdrasill, the World Tree. The sacred tree of the Norse gods." She shook her head. "I don't think she wanted to give my voice back."

"Wow. I've heard of the World Tree with roots firmly embedded in the Earth and branches that reach the sky. How did you manage to travel that far on your human legs, much less obtain that feather?"

"Astrid refused to let me travel alone. She said I'd need her assistance communicating with everyone on my journey. So, we *borrowed* two ponies from the far pasture that shouldn't be missed and headed out at dawn in the general direction of the World Tree."

Rungnir shivered and waves pummeled the shore. "You are so brave. What happened once you arrived?"

"I must admit I was afraid. The World Tree dwarfs everything around it."

"Anyone would be afraid. Even me, big as I am."

"We camped beneath its branches, then walked around its trunk searching for a fallen eagle feather. It took us two days and we found nothing. Its closest branches were too far to reach, so climbing it was out of the question. I wasn't sure what to do."

The Little Mermaid paused as if she were reliving the experience in her mind. "Thankfully, I spied Ratatoskr, the squirrel that carries messages between the eagle at the top of the tree and Nidhoggr, the dragon that lives far beneath it. Astrid relayed my story to the soft-hearted squirrel and asked if he would give the eagle my message. Ratatoskr agreed and climbed until he was nothing more than a tiny speck on the side of the tree. Days later, he returned, bearing a message and one pristine white feather."

"What was the message?"

"It went something like this: 'Little mermaid, you have traveled far and dealt with great hardship in the name of love. Eagles love deeply and mate for life, so I can sympathize with your desire to win your prince. I award you one of my sacred feathers and wish you Godspeed.'"

"Did you make it back in time to get your voice back and tell the prince he'd made a huge mistake?"

The Little Mermaid's chin quivered, and her eyes dropped to her lap. She brushed away a tear with her hand. "Yes and no. By the time we returned, wedding guests had already begun to partake in the week-long festivities. Both families were jovial and pleased with the union. And the bride-to-be and the prince beamed with happiness. It was clear he'd fallen in love with her."

"Ouch."

"I couldn't disrupt their happiness. How could I marry him knowing he loved someone else? I gave the witch her feather in return for my voice. Clearly, she didn't anticipate my success. But she honored our agreement. Then, I asked her to make me a mermaid once more."

"And didn't she? You certainly look the part. I mean, you have the tail and all."

She sighed. "No, not yet. In case you haven't guessed by now, mine isn't a happily-ever-after fairytale."

"I get that. Go on."

"The sea witch said I had to perform an additional task. Only then would she return me to my mermaid state."

"What was it this time?"

"I had to procure a magical amulet from the goddess Idunn that would make its wearer eternally young and beautiful."

Rungnir snorted through his gills. "Oh, great. You mean that sea witch is going to be around until Doomsday?"

A smile flitted across The Little Mermaid's face.

"So, how did you manage to talk Idunn into it? I wouldn't even know how to approach an Asgard goddess."

"Idunn is also the keeper of apples. I remembered that Loki, the god of mischief, once lured Idunn away from Asgard by telling her he'd found apples that rivaled hers. One of Astrid's kin works in

Idunn's orchards. He let it slip that unusual apples were being produced near the North Sea—red-skinned sea apples with fleshy blue fruit that tasted of honey mead with a hint of spice. I prepared them by injecting blue dye and mead into the largest apples I could find and polished them until I could see my image in them."

"Clever."

"Mmm. Astrid advised me to disguise myself as the sea witch so Idunn would take her wrath out on the witch once she discovered the deception. So I waited in the shallow waters by the shore, wearing a gray wig and black cape, with a basket piled high with apples. Before long, Idunn appeared."

Rungnir's mouth formed a perfect O. "Wow. I've never seen a real goddess. What did she look like?"

"She wore a garland in her golden hair that reached to the ground. A golden glow shimmered around her, and she vibrated with beauty and vitality. I couldn't peel my eyes off her. She asked me what I wanted for the entire basket. I had barely responded when she snapped her fingers, held out her palm, and, like magic, a hawk dropped the amulet in it. She handed it to me and reached for the basket of apples. And then. . ."

"And then?"

The Little Mermaid squirmed like a schoolgirl caught in a lie. "I couldn't go through with it. It was dishonest and deceitful. I returned the amulet to her, tore off my disguise, and told her my story. Her countenance grew dark and stone-like. I feared she might strike me dead right there. But I plunged ahead, and eventually her face softened and her darkness faded. She recited a spell over the amulet and handed it to me."

'Give this to the sea witch,' she said. 'It will transform her temporarily so you can become a mermaid once more and go back to your family and your world.' I returned to the shore by the prince's castle and met with the sea witch. She clasped the pendant around her neck, and true to her word, turned me into a mermaid once more."

"So what are you doing here? I mean, I'm happy you're here, but why didn't you go home right then?"

The Little Mermaid's face grew splotchy and tears escaped from her eyes. "The prince and his bride saw me before I could leave. Once they were married, she confessed to the prince that I had rescued him. The prince wanted to show me his gratitude by holding a huge banquet in my honor. I couldn't refuse, even though it would delay my departure. Finally, it was time to go. I leapt with joy from the rock to the sea below, diving deeper and deeper, enjoying pain-free movement and the ocean on my skin once again. But I soon realized I couldn't breathe. I panicked and barely make it back to the surface. The sea witch awaited me."

'You didn't think I'd believe you without testing the amulet, did you? I put it around a ripe apple and waited to see what would happen. It was fresh for a week or so. Then it shriveled and the flesh began to rot. Thanks to your duplicitous act, you can now breathe on land but your mertail will render you virtually immobile, and you can swim in the sea but you can't breathe underwater.'

The Little Mermaid shivered, then continued. "She started to leave when I grabbed her dress to stop her and apologized to her profusely for my deception. I begged her to give me another chance."

"And did she agree?"

"Yes, *if* I completed two more tasks. First, Idunn had to remove the limiting spell from the amulet so the witch could enjoy everlasting beauty and youthfulness. That was the easy one. Idunn was so smitten with the idea of blue sea apples, she created some for herself. She happily granted my request." Her eyes looked bleak. "But I can't possibly complete the final task."

"I'm sure whatever it is you'll be able to accomplish it. You succeeded with the others."

The Little Mermaid's shoulders sagged, and her head drooped. "It's too hard. For this task I must tell the sea witch when and where King Njor, the god who rules over the sea, will visit Earth."

"Whatever for?"

"Revenge against the prince. She plans to seduce King Njor and become queen of the high seas, not just 'a dilapidated, ancient land castle.' Her words, not mine."

"Whoa. No way. Poor King Njor."

"He lives in a palace in Asgard, but every century or two he comes down to Earth and swims along the seashore. Only The Nine Daughters of Aegir know when and where that will be. I must find out his schedule and give it to her."

"Why doesn't she do it herself?"

The Little Mermaid rolled her eyes. "She had a fling with one of their mates. She's no longer welcome." She dropped her head to her chest. When she raised it, Rungnir noticed tears in her eyes. "She might as well have asked me to fly to the moon. I'm no longer a mermaid. There's no way I can locate the Nine Daughters unless they happen to swim along the shore right under my nose."

Rungnir's arms and legs started bouncing around in different directions. Finally, something he could do to show The Little Mermaid how much he cared for her. "You can if I help. I can ask around. Sea creatures will tell me because they are terrified of me. Once I find the Nine Daughters, I'll do whatever it takes to find out his schedule."

The Little Mermaid's eyes lit up. "You'd do that for me?"

Rungnir's skin turned crimson. "Of course. What are friends for? You stay here and I'll be back before you know it."

As the leaves began to fall, The Little Mermaid despaired that Rungnir had forgotten her. One evening, when she had almost given up hope, he appeared.

She clapped her hands, eyes shining like precious jewels. "You're back and safe. Did you find the Nine Daughters?"

"I did. And I have the information you need."

Her smile rivaled the brilliant sunset. "Now I can summon the sea witch, give her the information, and she'll turn me into my original form. I'll be able to swim the high seas and the oceans once more."

From under a rock, she collected the small pouch the witch had given her and threw its contents into the waters which began to bubble up and shimmer in hues of the rainbow. Immediately the sea witch appeared.

"You have what I requested?"

The Little Mermaid nodded, barely containing her excitement.

The sea witch's eyes locked on hers. "For real, this time? No tricks?"

"No tricks. Tell her, Rungnir."

"King Njord will arrive on the shores of the Baltic Sea this coming spring. He'll be taking requests from seafolk then. That's when you can see him."

The Little Mermaid swallowed hard. "Now, will you return me to my former state?"

The sea witch produced a vial from her bag. "Here. Drink this. Every last drop. Then you'll be able to live in the sea once more."

The Little Mermaid took the vial in her hand and slowly raised it to her lips, then set it on a rock.

"What's the matter? It's a perfectly fine potion. I made it fresh this morning."

"How do I know it isn't poison? Or that it won't turn me into a toad?"

Rungnir winced.

The sea witch pursed her lips together and narrowed her eyes. "Do you have a choice?"

The Little Mermaid's chin trembled. "No." She picked up the vial again and swallowed the potion.

"But be warned, mermaid. If I find out your *friend*—she nodded in Rungnir's direction—has deceived me, you'll both be sorry you ever met me." She started to leave, then turned back and pointed one finger at The Little Mermaid. "And I don't want to see you come anywhere near King Njord. Is that clear?"

"Perfectly."

The Little Mermaid and the Kraken waited a few minutes until the sea witch was far beneath the sea.

Rungnir dropped his head to his chest and drew his tenacles close to his body. "So, going to join your family and friends, now?" he asked in a flat, monotone voice.

In response, The Little Mermaid dove into the waters where the North Sea and the Baltic Sea merge and swam in circles under the sea. She looked back at the lonely Kraken, who had submerged but stayed where he was. "Well, aren't you coming with me?"

Rungnir's arms and legs tangled together and he almost turned a somersault in his haste to reach her. "Yes. Yes, of course."

The Little Mermaid swam up to him. "You are my best friend, Rungnir. I want to spend this special day with you. No one but you. You've stood by me and encouraged me since the day we met. For now, let's swim the ocean waters I've missed so much under the starlight. You can meet my family tomorrow."

So, did The Little Mermaid and Rungnir the Kraken live happily ever after? That, my friend, is a tale for another day.

KERFUFFLE OVER THE NORWEGIAN SEA

JIM TRITTEN

"Jimmy, how you doin'?" Jack shook my hand. We were in the Reno, Nevada hotel meeting room that would serve as our reunion headquarters for the next three days. Whenever I hear Jack come into sight, he always says the same thing: "Jimmy, how you doin'?" No one else that I know ever calls me "Jimmy," but Jack always uses that diminutive for some reason. Not that I mind it – after all, that is what most people called me through high school. I cannot see Jack or hear his familiar voice call me Jimmy without thinking about one night fifty years earlier in September 1972, a night that is seared into my brain forever.

We both sit down; I give Jack a bottle of cold beer and go through the old ritual of getting out my old dark blue Navy pilot's flight logbook and thumbing through the drying and yellowing pages. We do this every reunion. There it is, September 26th. The line entry in the record written in red ink. A flight in a Stoof, the unofficial name for an S-2G "Tracker," Bureau Number 152811, 5.8 hours total flight time, 4 hours of night time, 4 hours of actual instrument conditions, and an actual radar approach and landing in Bodø, Norway. And it shows that Jack and I flew together on that fateful evening. Suddenly, I am no longer in a Reno hotel room but instead north of the Arctic Circle over the Norwegian Sea in our twin-engine carrier-based Navy aircraft.

~

"Jimmy, let's climb up and get some altitude." As soon as I advanced the throttles, there was a series of loud bangs and milder pops. Then the cockpit filled with flashes of light, white smoke, and the smell of burned aviation gasoline and oil. I looked at the red-lit gauges in the dark cockpit and saw that the port engine tachometer was falling off, showing that it was not developing full power. I instinctively throttled back the left engine until the popping stopped and turned the aircraft east towards the nearest land and a safe long runway ashore. "Jack, I'm headed to the beach."

Jack, sitting in the right seat as co-pilot, was a Lieutenant Commander. He was both one grade senior in rank to me and actually pilot in command of the flight. That meant that Jack would be making all official decisions about the flight. Although both of us were fully qualified aircraft commanders, we had been scheduled together so that Jack could conduct my annual instrument check. I was sitting in the left seat and performing first pilot duties while Jack in the right seat functioned as co-pilot although really in charge. Jack and I had known each other for some time and normally got along without any problems. But he was the boss and we both knew it.

Jack radioed USS Intrepid (CVS-11): "We've got a rough running port engine, and we're headed to the beach." After a slight pause, the air controller replied: "Negative, return to the ship for a landing. Your signal is Charlie 30" (indicating that we should expect to land in about thirty minutes). Despite my instincts and with no order from Jack, I turned back in the rain and dark towards the west and the aircraft carrier. We were given radar vectors and then told to hold until the flight deck was cleared of other aircraft so that we could make a landing.

New and even louder bangs and pops filled our eardrums and the cockpit once again filled with flashes of light, acrid smells, and white smoke. Both of us flinched in our seats and involuntarily took in sudden breaths. Then without any actions by either of us, one tremendous "BANG" caused the whole aircraft to shudder as yellow, and red flames shot out the front of the port engine through the slowly rotating propeller. "Shit," we both said as we looked out the left side. I pulled back and to the right on the controls as the aircraft pitched down and yawed to the left. Engine sounds diminished, and blue flames out of the exhaust stacks died completely.

Our speed slowed, and the altimeter began to unwind. I increased rudder pressure on the right foot pedal as the aircraft's remaining engine responded to my throttle movements forward to generate more power that would keep us in the air.

"Jack, we've lost number one, and I've got to feather it."

Since Jack was legally in charge, I did not automatically feather the propeller but instead informed him that is what we needed to do while I awaited his concurrence. Making a decision to feather a windmilling propeller attached to a dead engine was a no-brainer. Without moving the propeller blades into a streamlined position and reducing the drag, we would descend and eventually hit the water.

Per standard operating procedures, Jack and I both agreed on which of the two engines was causing the problem and which over-head button would cause the dead prop to feather. I pushed the correct [left] red feather button, causing the three propeller blades to align themselves with the wind stream so that we could maintain altitude and airspeed despite the loss of port power.

"Jack, we really ought to go to the beach." Beach the universal term used by sailors to refer to anywhere ashore. I don't think there are any actual sandy beaches along the treacherous Norwegian coastline.

Without waiting for a reply, I turned the yoke to bank the aircraft again the second time towards the east. We had taken off from the ship a little over an hour before. When our Stoof was catapulted into the air, the 872-foot-long gray aircraft carrier had been pitching and rolling with white foam coming over the bow. The gale winds were so strong that white foam and spray hit the aircraft parked behind the island amidships – more than a football field in length aft of the bow. We also knew after we had taken off, the sun had set, and a cold front had moved in, further agitating the ocean. Steady rain now fully obscured the moon and stars. Outside of the cockpit, everything was gray. There was no way to assess the air and sea boundary.

Jack radioed the ship: "We've lost the port engine, and we're headed to the beach." The ship replied with a simple acknowledgement, "Roger." I jettisoned the aircraft's antisubmarine warfare ordnance load to lighten the plane and calculated roughly how long it would take us to get to the closest divert airfield – Bodø, Norway – about two and a half hours east with a tailwind. The ship then radioed a "Request you return – your signal Charlie upon arrival." Not a direct order but clearly what they wanted. Come back to the ship and land here. I looked at Jack and knew what he was thinking.

We were scheduled to finish our major multinational naval exercise in the morning, and the ship was due in England the following evening. Having a broken plane stuck in Norway would prove to be a bit of a logistical and maintenance problem with the rest of the air wing a thousand miles away. Jack was one of the department heads in our squadron, and he wanted to get back and do things that senior officers always felt they needed to do in person. "Jimmy, we need to go back to the ship…" Again, not an order, but close enough. I saw him looking at me and knew he meant it. I banked the aircraft again to the west, and we closed the distance to the carrier – now about a half hour away.

Instead of listening to his every word, all I could think about was how tough it was going to be to land our plane with only one working engine onboard a heaving deck, in a gale, and the pitch dark.

Jack added, "…Jimmy, I really want to get back aboard tonight."

On the other hand, I was flying the plane, and I was very skeptical of this course of action. I considered my words carefully as I responded, "Jack, if you really want to land this broke-ass airplane aboard the ship tonight, get into the left seat and do it yourself." Probably not the most diplomatic way to speak to a senior officer who would control my career with remarks he made later about my conduct on this flight.

Before he could reply, I put my finger on the radio transmit button and asked the ship to let me talk to one of the landing signal officers (LSOs). These were fellow pilots trained to help up during the final stage of landings at sea. To my relief, one of my fellow junior officers and good friends came on the radio. I asked him directly: "Paddles (the universal call sign for the LSO), how's the deck?" I knew I could count on him to describe the actual conditions of the sea and the pitching and rolling of the deck at that moment without any editing from the senior officers also listening to the radio chatter and providing him with what they thought ought to be his answer.

There was an abnormally long pause before Paddle's very crisp and abnormal monotone answer came through our helmet earphones: "Smooth as glass."

"BULLSHIT" both Jack and I exclaimed without hitting the transmit button. There was no way in the world that the Norwegian Sea had gone from gale conditions a few hours ago to "smooth as glass." Those were probably the words from a senior officer (heavy) on the ship advising the LSO junior officer what he should say. Not those exact words, but suggesting the LSO tell us that conditions were good enough to get aboard. By transmitting "smooth as glass," the LSO sent us a message that those words were not his.

"Jimmy, you're right, let's go to the beach. There's no way that ship is not rocking and rolling in this weather."

I smiled and turned the aircraft again to the east and an airfield that was not bobbing up and down in a storm.

Before you take off on a carrier, the pilots are briefed on the direction and distance to the nearest divert airfield – just in case. We knew that was Bodø, Norway, and they would be remaining operational status while there was any chance that one of the aircraft participating in the NATO exercise might need to land ashore. To transit over the Norwegian Sea from where we got airborne from Intrepid to Bodø was going to take two and a half hours. If we lost the one remaining engine, or something else happened during that flight that would cause us to go into the water meant certain death. There were no ships along the way to come to our aid. If we survived a water crash, we would undoubtedly die from exposure within minutes. Not a great course of action, but better, I thought, than trying to land on a pitching deck in a storm at night with less than complete control of the aircraft. On the other hand, if we went into the water trying to land aboard Intrepid, there were helicopters and escort surface ships to come to our aid and attempt to pluck us out of the freezing Norwegian Sea before hypothermia set in. Tough choice.

Despite frequent continued calls from the ship's controllers, our squadron commander, and several other heavies to "please" come and at least try to land on the ship, we kept flying east. I sensed that if we tried to land on the ship, we would burn up so much fuel that we would no longer have enough aviation gasoline to fly ashore just in case things got worse. Not a good situation.

We were picked up by Norwegian military radar and got a steer to Bodø. Our broken Stoof droned on toward the rugged Nordland coastline in the dark, the rain, and with only the one engine keeping us in the air and out of the frigid turbulent sea. The Norwegian controllers tried to keep up our spirits with occasional chatter about what to expect upon arrival. We learned that Bodø only had one landing strip oriented roughly west from the sea to the east with jagged mountains to the north and further east.

On final approach with the runway lights visible, the Norwegian tower controller informed us: "Bodø has rainstorms in all quadrants with winds gusting from variable directions but generally from the west-northwest." That meant the winds would be behind and to the left of us when we touched down. A quick calculation revealed that the crosswind that evening was outside the design specifications of our Stoof. The book said we could not execute a safe asymmetrical single-engine landing with winds coming from the side of the dead engine. In addition, I would not be able to generate sufficient thrust with just the one good engine to get airborne again once we had touched down and if we then had another problem. Also, even if Jack and I both pushed on the right rudder pedal, would we be able to generate the muscle strength needed to manhandle the asymmetry of the one good engine? It was going to be a straight shot in from the west over the Norwegian Sea with only one chance at bringing this crippled bird down safely.

"Jack, this is not going to be pretty – follow me on the controls and back me up." My stomach tightened, and my jaws clenched.

I lowered the landing gear at the last moment to not further exacerbate drag, making flight even more difficult. As I lined up on final approach with our landing light shining ahead through the rain, I could see the green runway threshold lights and the white striping on the tarmac at the approach end coming closer as we lowered down towards *terra firma*. The wheels touched down one at a time on the dark pavement, and the white runway lights on either side flashed by way too fast. The rear quartering wind pushed us down the runway more quickly than we wanted instead of a normal landing into the wind, which would slow us down. I throttled back to idle on the good starboard engine. I saw the red overrun lights at the far side of the field rapidly approaching. The brakes had no effect on the rain-soaked tarmac as we thundered ahead, not slowing much.

A sudden gust from the north caught the tail. The plane weather-cocked violently to the left. "Shit." We were going down a wet runway with the tires hydroplaning on top of the water but not gripping the surface. Worse, the tires were not rolling in the direction of our travel – the wheels were cocked about forty-five degrees to the left of the direction of travel. As we skidded off the runway, I began to see distant blue taxiway lights and nothing but blackness in front of me.

"J-I-I-I-M-M-M-Y-Y-Y, you got this aircraft under control?"

I didn't reply. I was too busy stomping on the brakes, kicking the rudder pedals, and bracing for a crash.

Fortunately, it was either not our time, or Jack and I had cashed in on some good karma. After leaving the runway and being enveloped in the darkness, the plane rolled over level dirt and wet grass, and we finally slowed to a very welcome stop.

I cut the fuel and ignition to the starboard engine, and there were no mechanical sounds for the first time in hours. Jack and I sat there, immobile, and speechless. Our flight suits were soaking wet, but we were alive.

After what seemed like an eternity, I exited the aircraft on not too steady legs. Jack and I sat on the wet ground under the starboard wing and sucked in the welcome, clean cold Norwegian mist. The sound of sirens from the crash trucks grew louder as they closed to our position, red lights flashing and deep-throated diesel engines racing.

I looked up towards the tower. There was a Scandinavian Airlines System (SAS) jetliner on the airfield's parking area only a few hundred feet away from where we had ungracefully ceased moving but on a direct path ahead. The boarding ramp on the SAS jet was still down, and its engines did not appear to be running.

Without saying a word, I got up, trotted over to the airliner, and walked up the ramp.

Five minutes later, I slowly walked back to our broken-down aircraft and Jack, grinning widely – with eight frosty cold bottles of Tuborg beer.

～

"Well, Jack, is that the way you remember it?" Jack shakes his head and says, "Jimmy, we only made the one turn back to the ship, and I always agreed with you that we should go to the beach."

"Bullshit Jack," I insisted as we both laughed and drank a nice cold bottle of Tuborg to the memory of the LSO who, by telling us the sea was "smooth as glass," was actually telling us there was no way in hell we were going to safely get aboard the ship that one night on the storm-ravaged Norwegian Sea. And who had saved our asses.

～

EPILOGUE:

Some weeks after my return to the ship, I received the following citation from the Commander, Antisubmarine Warfare Group FOUR, at an awards ceremony held in our squadron ready room aboard Intrepid.

"For outstanding performance of duty on 26 September 1972 as a Carrier Antisubmarine Plane Commander in Air Antisubmarine Squadron TWENTY-SEVEN, while deployed on board USS Intrepid (CVS-11) in the Norwegian Sea. While airborne on an antisubmarine mission in exercise STRONG EXPRESS, Lieutenant TRITTEN's aircraft experienced a power loss and subsequent failure of the port engine. Complicating this emergency situation was the fact that weather and sea conditions were moderately severe, resulting in diversion to a distant and unfamiliar landing field under conditions of darkness. Post flight inspection of the failed engine revealed that Lieutenant TRITTEN's timely and correct securing of the engine had prevented further engine damage, allowing rapid repair and return of the aircraft to operational status within less than thirty-six hours. By his outstanding airmanship and superior technical knowledge, Lieutenant TRITTEN reflected great credit upon himself, his squadron and the United States Naval Service."

G.L. CASSELL
Rear Admiral, U.S. Navy
Commander Antisubmarine Warfare Group FOUR

A shorter and earlier version was originally published as "Night Flight to Norway," in the *Corrales Writing Group 2013 Anthology*, Sandi Hoover, Tom Neiman, Don Reightley, Jim Tritten, Patricia Walkow, Leon Wiskup, North Charleston, SC: CreateSpace, October 2013, pp. 107-113. Another version with photographs appeared with an Italian aviation online publisher as "The story of a U.S. Navy S-2 Tracker that lost one engine, at night, in bad weather, off Norway," January 23, 2015, http://theaviationist.com/2015/01/23/s-2-flying-to-norway/. This digital version was awarded an Honorable Mention, Feature Story, Online Publication in the New Mexico Press Women 2016 Communications Contest.

MEETING JAWS

PAUL MILA

October 18, 2019, Guadalupe Island, the eastern Pacific, a volcanic island about 160 miles off the west coast of Mexico's Baja California Peninsula.

I take an extra breath from my regulator, just to make sure it's delivering sufficient air, before the water closes over my head. A few seconds later and a couple of feet deeper, the sea completely envelops me. The cool Pacific water, low 60 degrees, seeps into my 7-mil wetsuit, twice as thick as a light-weight Caribbean wetsuit designed for warmer water. I'm chilled until the wetsuit traps the water and my body warms the water against my skin. I'm also wearing a neoprene hood and gloves to retain as much heat as possible. Cool water sucks the heat from your body 25 times faster than cool air, so hypothermia is a risk.

While our shark cage slowly descends, I grab the bars and test them, pushing and pulling as hard as I can. I recall the scene from *Jaws*, where a great white shark tore apart the anti-shark cage that oceanographer Matt Hooper (Richard Dryfuss) used. That did not end well! These bars are thick, firm, and seem strong, but still I wonder, *what if*. We reach our planned depth of 30 feet, and the cage jerks to a halt. My feet are firmly planted to the bottom of the cage, thanks to the 40 pounds of lead in my weight vest. I normally carry about 12-14 pounds when I dive so I'm neutrally buoyant. But in this case, the crew does not want us floating around inside the cage. They explained, ". . . because that's when accidents happen." *What kind of accidents,* I wondered, but did not ask. Compressors on the boat feed air to us through hoses. I glance at the corner of the cage and I see an emergency air tank and regulator secured to the bars, one for each diver. They explained, ". . . in case the air hose snaps." Or, I wonder, gets ripped apart by a shark? *I guess that's one of the possible accidents?*

There isn't too much to do while waiting for the great whites to show up, so I check my camera settings, and think about what has led me to this intersection with an apex predator. Looking into the depths, I notice a dark torpedo shape begin to materialize, rising out of the blue gloom. I wonder what will happen next.

The desire to meet JAWS up close and personal began after diving with Caribbean reef sharks in Nassau, Bahamas in 2002 (without cages), and then several years later after a day's shark cage diving from a boat called the *Sea Turtle,* based out of Montauk Long Island. We saw and dived with several blue sharks and a curious mako. Watching these graceful predators in their natural environment was exhilarating. I knew great whites were next on my bucket list.

There are only a couple of places in the world where you are sure to encounter great whites in clear water, and can do so safely: South Africa, Australia, and Guadalupe Island, Mexico. Guadalupe Island was the closest to Long Island, so the choice was easy. However, sometimes "life" gets in the way. By 2018 I still hadn't made it to Guadalupe. But diving in Cozumel, Mexico in December 2018, I met Paul Kern, who was diving with our group. Paul had just returned from diving with the great whites at Guadalupe Island, with an outfit called *Nautilus Adventures.* Regaling us with stories about his adventure and showing us his amazing shark photos was the catalyst I needed. As soon as I returned home from Cozumel, I contacted acclaimed underwater photographer, Richard Salas, who I had met on a previous dive trip to Cozumel. I had learned Richard was putting together an expedition with *Nautilus Dive Adventures* the following October to photograph great whites. So, I contacted Richard and booked my flight.

The plan involved flying from New York to San Diego to meet the *Nautilus Dive Adventures* group, and 18 other shark enthusiasts, including 10-year-old Logan. Logan's mom did not realize that her dive instructor husband was taking their son on a great white shark diving adventure until she dropped them off and met the group. To say she was not pleased with her husband when she learned about our itinerary would be a serious understatement! Logan was all up for the challenge, so mom grudgingly accepted the fact as business as usual. I got the definite impression that their family dynamics had all the makings for a great TV sitcom!

We boarded a comfortable coach bus for a three-hour ride to Ensenada, Mexico where our dive boat, The 105-foot *Undersea Hunter* was berthed. We enjoyed a group dinner and then boarded the *Hunter*. We slipped out of Ensenada harbor in the early evening, and after enjoyable conversations learning about each other's backgrounds and dive experiences, we retired to our berths listening to the rumble of the *Hunter's* engines.

Paul Mila photo ©

Two details that I had not counted on made the voyage to Guadalupe Island challenging. First, the *Undersea Hunter* was an old boat, launched in 1968. The boat was a diving legend, featured in many old South Pacific IMAX underwater movies. It was modernized in 2017, but still only had a cruising speed of about ten knots. Second, while Guadalupe Island is 160 miles directly west of the Mexican coast, our trip leaving north from Ensenada, was about 250 miles.

This meant an overnight voyage of at least 24 hours on the open sea. Most people don't travel on the ocean totally out of sight of land unless they're on a large cruise ship. The open ocean is a different "animal" from the ocean most of us experience closer to shore. The force of the unimpeded eight-to ten-foot ocean waves we encountered tossed our 105-foot vessel around like a cork. To make matters worse, we didn't face the waves head-on. Instead, they kept striking us from the side (a "beam sea," in nautical lingo), so the *Undersea Hunter* was constantly rolling side-to-side for hours. The next morning, I awoke to the sight of an angry ocean outside my waterline porthole.

Paul Mila photo ©

Even the strongest stomachs among us did not fare well during the crossing. I was lucky; the only thing I lost was my appetite! After a full day of rocking and rolling on a rough sea, we arrived in the sheltered cove of Guadalupe Island at around 10:00 pm the following evening. Those who could eat, had a light dinner. Then, we prepared to meet the great white sharks early tomorrow morning.

Daylight provided my first view of Guadalupe Island. It was stark and foreboding, a craggy volcanic island, with no vegetation. It appeared lifeless except for nesting seabirds flying above, and a seal colony (shark food) sunning themselves at the rocky base. My first great white sighting was from the safety of our boat's rear deck diving platform, where three dive cages, port, starboard and stern, were located. Two crew members standing on platforms extending out over the water chummed to attract sharks. They used ten-to-fifteen-pound frozen tuna chunks attached to ropes without hooks, for the safety of the sharks. Soon, we saw a dorsal fin break the surface, much like the conning tower of a submarine emerging from the deep. We watched the tall fin approach, propelled by the rhythmic swaying of the shark's tail (caudal fin). Then, the dorsal fin slipped below the surface and all was quiet. We stared at the water, expectantly. Soon, a chumming crew member cried out: "He's coming!"

Suddenly, the surface exploded in a foamy frenzy. The tuna was clamped sideways in the jaws of what resembled a set of Hoffritz steak knives! The great white's quick, powerful head-shake ripped the tuna from the rope. The violence of the attack was so exhilarating that everyone cheered. As the shark crossed our stern someone shouted, "Look at the size of that dorsal fin!"

Paul Mila photo ©

In the few seconds before the shark returned to the deep with its breakfast tuna-snack, I tried to estimate the size of a shark sporting a three- to-four-foot-tall dorsal fin. My meditation was broken by one of the crew members. "Okay, Paul, you're next in the cage!" Several minutes later, another cage-mate and I suited up and we prepared to meet JAWS.

Richard Salas photo ©

So now two of us are inside a cage, thirty feet deep. The bottom here is about 300 feet to a shelf below, and then slopes down off the shelf to over 1,000 feet. The visibility is excellent, gin-clear, exceeding 100 feet. Soon, we watch a ghostly apparition slowly take shape. My heart rate accelerates as I realize this is the real thing, not an image on celluloid. My first impression is that the great white's countershading (darker on top so it is difficult to see from above, and lighter on the bottom to blend in with the lighter surface when viewed from below) is remarkably effective. If I had been a seal lounging at the surface it would have been game over, very quickly. I'm wondering what the shark will do when it realizes two tasty morsels are dangling above. It approaches and then passes below the cage. The shark appears to be about twelve-to-fifteen-feet in length. I can see that this is not a mind-less predator but a cautious hunter, inspecting the situation to deter-mine the safety and probability of a successful attack. It circles again, then passes over us. With its pectoral fins extended, this great white reminds me of a jumbo jet – with teeth!

Paul Mila photo ©

We keep watching as the predator circles our cage, and then approaches us for a closer peek at the delectable goodies inside. Being evaluated as suitable food by a great white shark is very unsettling, even from the safety provided by thick metal bars. I have looked into the eyes of whales and dolphins. They express curiosity, intelligence, perhaps even humor. These eyes are very different. They are dark, cold and hard. There is intelligence behind their deadly stare, but the evaluation process is simple, providing the shark's brain with the information it needs to survive: is this food, a threat, or just part of the background?

Paul Mila photo ©

Soon, the shark is joined by another, also about twelve-to-fifteen feet in length. We watch these graceful predators circling, approaching, and occasionally lunging at the surface for a juicy chunk of tuna-on-a-rope. After about forty minutes the cage is raised to give other divers their time observing and photographing these magnificent animals. The schedule for the next several days is at least three dives per day inside either the descending cages on either side of the boat, or inside the stern cage which remains tethered to the boat just below the surface. We soon learn that the surface cage provides better opportunities for action photos than the deep cages as the sharks lunge for the tuna chum.

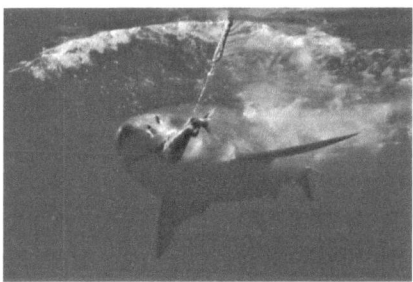

Paul Mila photo ©

Paul Mila photo ©

One day, expedition leader Rich Salas joins me in the cage, and I am fortunate that he takes a shot of me photographing a great white as it circles us. This may sound strange to those planning for a long life and lengthy retirement, but my hope for the next three days of our adventure is to photograph great whites up close, charging and bumping our cage with razor-sharp teeth flashing.

Richard Salas photo ©

All too soon, the last day of our adventure arrives. We only have the morning and the early afternoon to dive before we pull up anchor and depart Guadalupe Island. I've taken a lot of great shots, but not the photo I'm after. I want that toothy closeup. I want to experience the power of a great white pounding our cage. That's when "Big Mama" shows up. The same sharks show up year after year at Guadalupe Island, so the crew members recognize them by various markings and scars, and name them. They keep a photo-scrapbook, which they update every season as the sharks grow older and mature, and they can tell males from females. Male sharks have a set of "claspers," two external sex organs located on their underside, in front of their tail fin. They haven't seen Big Mama all year but now she has arrived, possibly to mate. She is close to twenty-feet in length, they estimate at least eighteen feet, and her girth is enormous.

Paul Mila photo ©

I jump into the stern cage with two other divers, and we start taking still-shots and video. I watch her pass another cage and then head for ours. I realize this is the moment I've been waiting for! I get my camera ready as she approaches, but sharks are unpredictable. As I'm ready to take *"THE"* shot, Big Mama suddenly swerves toward us and smashes into our cage, sending me onto my butt on the bottom of the cage as I press the shutter.

After Big Mama leaves, we exit our cage very excited by our close encounter with her. I review my shots and that's when I realize that my perfectly composed toothy head shot did not happen. But I did manage to get Big Mama as she smashed into our cage. It is not a great photo missing her eyes and teeth raking our cage, but the image provides a sense of her size and power.

Paul Mila photo ©

Several minutes after we shed our dive suits and dry off, the team leader shouts, "Ninety minutes, folks. Last chance before we leave." I'm tempted to suit up and jump back in, but I've had enough. We have experienced several days of amazing great white encounters, exceeding my expectations. An hour later, the crew hauls the cages out of the water and secures them on deck. We raise anchor and the *Undersea Hunter's* engines rumble to life. I watch the sun setting behind Guadalupe Island as we depart. I hope to return someday, and perhaps meet Big Mama again!

Paul Mila photo ©

ACROSS THE ATLANTIC

JASMINE TRITTEN

The Sea cures all ailments of man.

~ Plato

A dream or reality? Like a Nordic Viking Queen, I stood on the top deck of the Norwegian ocean liner, *Bergensfjord*, in the summer breeze, clutching Dannebrog – the Danish flag – in my right fist, ready to conquer the world. My armor? A cobalt blue skirt and jacket my mother had sewn with a matching, blue-dotted blouse, and white gloves she made me wear to protect the sensitive skin of my hands. The chilly wind blew through my blonde hair and erased memories of a time gone by. I had made the leap and headed into the unknown.

Family and friends clumped together on the quay of *Langelinie*, in the port of Copenhagen, near the famous statue of the Little Mermaid. They threw flowers my way, I heard laughter and cries simultaneously, and they swung flags, scarves, balloons, handkerchiefs, or signs with BON VOYAGE. While waving my arms back and forth with the Danish flag tight in my hand, I fought the tears and my stomach shuddered.

Never had I traveled on a large ship across the big ocean to another part of the world. But I remember having sailed in boats from Denmark to England, Germany, and Norway besides taking small ferries between the islands of my home country. However, nothing measured up to this voyage. My life would never be the same again. While bouncing from one foot to the other my heart raced in my chest. Next to me stood my Danish friend Lis, a schoolmate of mine, who at the last moment joined me in this adventure.

The amazing *Bergensfjord* happened to be one of the last transatlantic ocean liners in 1964 sailing from Copenhagen via Oslo to New York. Of the 878 passengers onboard, more than half were immigrants, including Lis and me. From the mid-sixties on, people who desired to travel from Copenhagen to America, flew by airplane straight to New York. Our ship appeared small and quaint compared to the gigantic cruise ships currently floating around every corner of the world containing 3,000-6,000 passengers. But not for me! I had never sailed in such an enormous vessel.

The ocean liner pulled away from my home country and set course to a new world. Fresh sea air saturated my nose and lungs and the loud band music faded from my ears. As the ship sailed further and further away from the dock, people gradually became smaller and smaller, turning into tiny dots in all colors of the rainbow until they became a big blur. I strained my eyes to get a last glimpse of them, then tears rolled down my cheeks from the excitement and exhilaration. Part of me felt sad because I still loved my family and friends. When would I ever see them again?

At that moment, saying goodbye to a world of twenty-one years became more difficult than anticipated. In hindsight, I left Denmark determined to experience other cultures and for adventure. My gut told me to leave, not my logical mind. While justifying my actions, Lis nudged me in the side and brought me back to reality. Glad she decided to come along after all.

Rays of the morning sun sparkled and danced on the surface of the ocean. I stared into the deep blue water rippling in a rhythmic pattern and then pulled off the white gloves from my hands. One at a time, I threw them into the rolling waves and watched them disappear. *The sea monster swallowed them. What a relief. Hurrah! I am free, free to be me. Free from my mother and her influence.* I leaned back my head, lifted my arms high and took in a deep breath, filling my lungs to their full capacity with the salty air from the sea.

Of course, I loved my mother, but needed to get away from her, as far away as possible, out of her clutch. My goal? San Francisco on the other side of the earth seemed like the perfect distance from Denmark. *I am now in control of my own future.* The vessel and ocean in front of my eyes steered me toward my destiny, whatever that might be. With an embroidered, ivory colored handkerchief I wiped away my tears, leaned towards Lis and said, "Do you think we'll ever return?"

She did not answer me right away. For a while we watched the waves splash as we walked along the side of the ship and looked back a last time at the country we had left behind. Cool mist from the white tops landed in my face, refreshed me, and cleared my head. Lis turned in my direction and said,

"Let's celebrate our freedom and our home for the next ten days." So, we headed down below into our cabin, lowered ourselves into small chairs, and gulped a shot of *aquavit* Lis brought. The potent liquid quickly ran through and warmed my body all the way to my toes, calming my emotions. I lay down and relaxed in the lower bunk bed.

Despite my dream finally coming true, tears welled up in my eyes, when I realized the monumental decision, I had made. *I wonder if I did the right thing.* Earlier in Denmark when I told my mother about my life-changing plans, she said to me, "Even if I don't like it, I would rather you go to America and be happy, than stay here unhappy." She gave me the green light to go. Forever I will remember her for that gift and have thanked her repeatedly ever since.

The next couple of days, we explored every square inch of the ship. Each time I walked along the decks on the outside and my eyes glanced at the shimmering surface of the cobalt blue water I felt invigorated. At the same time, as I gazed into the rolling waves, a healing took effect on my inner wounds and traumas, especially the trauma of my father's death when I was twelve years old...when my entire world collapsed. Here in the depth of the blues and foam of the ocean the buried feelings of despair drowned and dissipated.

As I leaned over the railing late one afternoon, my eyes skimmed over the white-topped surface towards the western horizon where the deep red setting sun cast its golden rays upon the sky. Thoughts and dreams of what awaited us in America swirled through my mind. Soon I would be in a different world. *How did the Vikings ever make it across the Atlantic Ocean in tiny boats with sails and oars? How many did not make it?*

Seagulls followed our ship. From the top deck, I threw pieces of leftover bread from our meals up into the sky and the gulls swooped around to catch them midair with their beaks. Each time I spotted gray and white Dolphins jump out of the water in front of the ship, I smiled. Gazing down into the darkness, I heard Frank Sinatra's voice singing "How Deep is the Ocean" repeatedly. I pondered the amount of Eiffel towers on top of each other it would take before reaching the bottom. The secrets of the sea stayed concealed. *I wonder the number of sunken ships with treasures lay underneath the surface, deep down at the bottom.*

When not with Lis, I sat on a bench outside on one of the top decks wrapped in a blanket and stared into the vastness, letting my imagination take me into another realm. *Maybe I will see the fin of a shark, or a whale jump out of the water.* I made up stories in my mind about what happened above the surface and about what took place beneath with fish and plants.

Often "The Little Mermaid" fairy tale by fellow Dane, Hans Christian Andersen, popped into my head. As a child, I sat on my father's knee while he read aloud about her adventures from under the sea. I still remember vividly two etchings of her from the leatherbound volume with her fishtail full of barnacles wrapped around seaweed at the bottom. *There is an entire world underneath the surface.* So, I fantasized about the bottom of the ocean. Fear never overwhelmed me during the long cruise. Like a true Viking I remained fearless and courageous.

Two young, naive, Danish, blue-eyed, blonde girls like Lis and me continuously had fun on the huge ship, even if most passengers were the same age as our grandparents. How could we help but flirt with the good-looking Norwegian crew onboard? Learning to say "no" to the constant offerings of drinks, became our biggest challenge. Besides refusing to indulge in the spreads of delicious Norwegian food served buffet style three times a day. When getting a whiff of smoked salmon or the strong aroma of European cheeses at the breakfast buffet, how could we resist the temptation?

To justify our ferocious appetites, we promenaded back and forth on the decks at all hours of the day. We dove into the large pool and swam unlimited laps to keep off the calories and used exercise machines in the gym. Every evening, the band played, and we danced our feet off. I pulled out on the dance floor each willing person to practice what I learned in Denmark of social dance, folk dance, or ballroom dance. The days ended singing with fellow Danes, songs we learned in our childhood, a treasured part of the Danish culture. *Would we remember our heritage, or might it become replaced with our new life in America?*

Then, suddenly a raging storm, like a hurricane, surprised us. For three days the ship rolled from one side to the other in waves as tall as two-story buildings. Half of the passengers became seasick and threw up. Most people stayed in their cabins dreadfully ill. Vomit boxes appeared everywhere. An unbearable stench filled the passageways and compartments, enough to make a person sick, even if you were not. The crew tied down tables and chairs. Rubber runners covered the floors to prevent people from sliding.

"We must stay strong through this," I hinted to Lis, determined not to give in to sickness. In that moment I truly felt like a Viking on my first voyage, embracing every moment whether good or bad. During the height of the storm, we stayed safe in our cabin, located mid-ship, lying down, holding on to our bunk beds. Earlier, I brought food to our cabin, enough to sustain us for a couple of days. Glad we had no window in our space. Unless we happened to be acrobats, walking around anywhere outside became impossible. Loud sounds hit our ears of crashing waves and objects flying, hitting whatever. Miraculously, we survived without getting ill or hurt. Must be our good Nordic genes.

After the horrendous storm everything became tranquil onboard for a couple of days. People slowly recovered from the tumultuous experience. Immediately, I went for a stroll on the freshly washed deck outside, stared into the relative calm water stretching as far as my eyes reached, into eternity, and thanked God for sparing us.

At sunrise as the fire red sun slowly ascended, the intoxicating smell of the ocean and the sound of waves crashing against the bow hypnotized me and brought back memories. Thoughts went back to my childhood when I watched the straight between Denmark and Sweden from my room in the villa where I lived the first twelve years of my life. I grew up next to water in which we swam and went sailing in the summer and ice skated in the winter, frequently in stormy weather.

About nine days passed, when in the long distance I spotted land, what looked like tall skyscrapers. As *Bergensfjord* approached New York City, my heart throbbed, and I smiled from one ear to the other. A big moment had arrived for this dream of mine. Our ship sailed up the Hudson River at sunset. We rushed straight up on the upper deck. With arms in the air and my lungs at full capacity I screamed,

"Hurrah, America, we are finally here!" People stared, but I did not care.

A red glow filled the evening sky and slowly changed into different shades of purple. Soon it darkened, and lights shined from all the buildings like stars. In awe, we reached for the luminosities but had to stay onboard until the following morning. Our ship slowly lowered its anchor for the night. *Cannot wait.* Hardly closed an eye. But we had one more hurdle before reaching land - before the end of our voyage.

Early the next morning, the lengthy process of entering the U.S. as immigrants began. Negative thoughts bombarded my head. *What if the Immigration and Naturalization officers do not accept us? They could refuse our entry and send us back to Denmark. The X-rays might show a spot on the lung suspicious of Tuberculosis. If we have visited The Soviet Union, been in jail or for whatever reason, they can just say "no."*

After standing in line for five hours onboard the ship to get on land in New York Harbor, my legs tired and my stomach quivered. Sweat dribbled down my back in the summer heat. I kept biting the insides of my cheeks until they bled. Under my left arm I carried a large, yellow, sealed envelope containing two chest X-rays. The bag over my right shoulder bulged with papers required for entry. For eight months prior to the trip, I went back and forth to process them at the American Embassy in Copenhagen.

Finally, my turn came. With a raising heart beat I stepped forward towards the immigration officer and smiled. Quickly he checked through my papers and X-rays without a word, and with a nod, let me go through. I sighed in relief and rubbed my tender shoulder muscles. *I cannot believe I went through already.*

Next in line, my friend Lis. The officer gazed at her papers, then lifted her X-rays up into the light. He rotated them, carefully examining every section from one side to the other. *Will he let her pass?* He frowned, pointed his finger to a spot on one of the X-rays and remarked,

"Something looks suspicious on the lung right there." I cringed. Lis spoke up at once, her voice shaking,

"I have had pneumonia twice, and it left scar tissue. That is what you see."

Surprised, the officer stared at her and examined the X-rays thoroughly one more time. Then he handed them back to her and shouted, "Okay, next person!" The sound of his loud voice hurt my ears, but we were free to go. *Yahoo! I cannot believe it is true.*

Grateful and relieved, we jumped up and down, each with a GREEN CARD in hand. After gathering papers and luggage we stepped triumphantly upon land while repeatedly shouting, "Hurrah, America, here we come."

From that time on, we had legal permission to stay in the U.S. for an unlimited time, on the condition we behaved ourselves. No more did we need to worry about falling in love with somebody and then having to leave the country after a certain period. The struggle had been long, with hurdles to overcome, but at last I was free to create my own life, free to be myself.

For years I lived an adventurous life in California and traveled around the world before I connected with my mother again. Despite living on opposite sides of the earth, we became closer than ever through letters and telephone conversations and repaired our once distraught relationship. To this day, I remain grateful she let me break free from her, from my home country and let me travel across the Atlantic Ocean toward my goal in America.

AT THE END OF MY ROPE

MICHAEL O'KEEFE

Piracy was my crime, and I would swing for it, a fitting end for a lucrative and violent career. How I got into this business was a bit more tangled; full of intrigue, world-hopping, and time travel. Though my punishment would be appropriate, I was a man out of time, existing beyond time's reckoning.

I was in the year of our Lord, 4529. Condemned to die, I was on the planet Aegina, in the Kepler solar system, to be hung by the neck by the Ministry of Justice of the Universal Democratic Monarchy. Yes, the universe has a king, and he doesn't like pirates. We were in Aegina's capital city of Casai Shima, but city is a misnomer. Aegina is comprised of 99.6 % water. The .4 % of land being small volcanic archipelagos and coral atolls. Casai Shima was where the Monarchy's forces caught up with me. So here is where I will hang.

Funny thing, a society that has perfected infinite ways to kill its sentient beings in an instant of unspeakable horror, it still chose to kill its pirates in the gruesome, old-fashioned way, just as it did on Earth since the first millennium. So, I would stretch at the end of a rope.

This wasn't the worst place to die. The gallows were situated on a bluff above Aegina's fine blue-sand beaches, overlooking the majestic Ochian Sea, where ocean mammals swam and played. The large blood-orange Kepler sun was warm on my face, the hot rays cooled by soft sea breezes. The two-headed gulls' melodious calls as they flew about the coast were like lullabies, accompanied by the waves cascading against the shore. My reverie was broken by the tread of the executioner climbing the stairs, the footfalls softer and lighter than I would have imagined. The hangman in black cloak and hood came from behind. The sweet smell of cinnamon and currants wafting forward and washing over me.

I was just fourteen when the beguiling Desdemona Kelly convinced me to flee with her from my beloved home of Dunfanaghy, on the coast of Donegal. She was only fifteen herself and already bored with the life of a girl in an Irish fishing village. Being 1649, she had little means of escape. But my Desi was a clever girl, bordering on diabolical. Of course, she found a way.

An enchantress, Desi's long thick red hair bounced behind her in cadence with her graceful movements, catching the sun and demanding I be enthralled. I was, from the first day I saw her. She smelled of cinnamon and currants, like warm soda bread fresh from the kiln. Tall, lithe yet curvaceous, with emerald eyes that snatched the soul right out of me, I would do her bidding until the ending of my days, which upon this scaffold, today seemed to be.

Following her like a devoted puppy, we stowed away on a ketch bound for Liverpool, making our way by foot and the occasional stolen horse to London. There we signed on to the crew of a galiot bound for Nassau in the Caribbean. The captain, a disgraced Royal Naval officer, had difficulty attracting a reputable crew, so he more than welcomed us.

Captain Percy Trevor was a privateer, taking prizes on behalf of the Crown, with a handsome cut for himself and his crew. Until King Charles was assassinated, touching off the English Civil War. All pretense of government cover was lost to us, and with it any reservation or compunction. The Golden Age of piracy began in that vacuum of order, and Captain Trevor was the most voracious pirate of the age.

Desi and I learned our trade at the knee of the master. No longer consigning ourselves to taking prizes from enemies of the Crown—what with no one wearing it—we raided everything that floated in those tropical waters. Trevor thought us naturals at mayhem. In truth, Desi was the natural. I was only skilled at complying with whatever she suggested, no matter how outrageous. While this resulted in my hands being saturated with blood, the lust for it was all hers. For me, all of that slaughter felt more like a gift to my beloved than murder. We were so rapacious; Trevor designated the two of us as his trusted first mates.

This exhilarating and thriving existence might have continued, but for Captain Trevor's affinity for the harlots. Coupled with copious amounts of rum, while ashore, all he did was drink and rut. It wasn't long before the *syph* took its toll, robbing him of all of his wits and much of his vigor.

"Percy has gone mad from his whore-mongering," Desi said.

"In this life, laid and crazy might not be a bad way to go," I observed.

"True enough," she said. "But the captain's poor judgment will likely take us down as well."

"What to do then, my love?"

"I think it's nigh-all time for a mutiny."

That is how Desdemona, and I became co-captains of the pirate ship Horrendous. Out of love for Desi and fear for myself, the crew fell in behind us. With her inspiration, I had become the most dreaded pirate on the seas, such a swath of murder and pillage had I cut. So, when I broached the subject of mutiny with the crew, I was met with nothing but fearful nods.

"The crew doesn't much speak to me," I said later to Desi.

"Because they're scared to death of you, Malachy," she laughed.

"Why would they be afraid of me?"

"You've killed more people than the bubonic plague."

"But that was work. Ordinarily, I'm a nice, easy-going *fella*."

"The crew doesn't think so. Did you know they called you *Black Malachy*?"

"They'd better call me *Captain* Black Malachy if they know what's good for 'em," I snarled.

We captained that ship for a few happy years, our lives enriched by bountiful helpings of rum, sodomy, and the lash. With no one to stop us, we were perfect scourges. Merchant ships and men-o-war alike saw our Jolly Roger flying from our mast in their nightmares—until 1658. With the Crown restored and a new governor of Nassau appointed, the regime focused the full power of the Royal Navy on our heads. When not raiding ships at sea, we spent the majority of our time running for our lives.

Panic is the bedfellow of risk, and we took too many. We sought shelter in the waters north of Puerto Rico, in the section of the Atlantic called the Bermuda Triangle. We thought fear and superstition would keep our pursuers at bay. We also believed His Majesty's sailors wanted nothing to do with the raging storm into which we sailed. We were correct on both counts, but events soon justified the superstition. There was more in those waters than rough currents and bad weather. With our sails struck and hatches battened, we sought to ride out the storm below.

"Do you think the ship will hold?" Desi asked.

"Oh sure," I said, confident the Horrendous could survive anything of this world.

But, beneath the waves was something not of this world at all. The Horrendous seemed to be snatched from the sea as if swallowed by a whale. We careened until the ship and all within it were suspended in thin air. We learned that this was just an effect of the enormous anti-gravity chamber within which we were trapped. The chamber was just one of many peculiar features of the colossal intergalactic pirate ship that snatched us up and flew into space. Our reality was explained by Captain Ivan Ratchakokov, commander of the pirate spaceship Groaza. His English was a halting thing; his accent similar to Russian, which we had only heard once and briefly from one of our crew on the Horrendous. We weren't sure what the Russian was saying. So, we killed him.

"*Dobro! You* ship and crew now our prize," the Captain said.

"Where are you taking us?" Desi demanded.

"Where not right question," he grunted. "When is better one."

Seeing our confusion, he explained.

"This ship not only travel between galaxies but do it in instant."

"Galaxies, you mean like other planets?" I asked.

"Not just other planets. But *all* planets."

The Captain paused to let that register.

"What did you mean by *when*?" Desi asked.

"To go so far, so fast, need to cross time. Moving now at one thousand times speed of light, to planet Carmora in year 3415."

"What?" Desi and I said, our minds thoroughly blown.

Captain Ratchakokov waved us off.

"No time to waste explaining things primitive minds can't understand. Right now, you have decision. Surrender and join us?"

"What if we don't?" Desi asked.

"Then you food for crew."

"You eat other people?" I asked, aghast.

"Technically, *people* is Earth term. Not many of crew from there. We actually whole other species—mostly same, but different. So, not cannibalism."

"It's still gross," Desi observed.

"Believe me," the captain snorted "Not many things in universe as savory as roast human. We discuss later—maybe not. For now, you join us for dinner, or you *be* dinner?"

In as much as we were in a futuristic spaceship, hurtling through time and the universe, we figured, what the hell? His awful English notwithstanding, Ratchakokov turned out to be a gracious host. He recognized our leadership qualities and welcomed us into his officer class. Our crew assimilated into the yeoman existence of the other space pirates.

The captain saw to our education as well. The science officer explained all of the technical marvels of the ship and the nuances of space-time navigation. The history officer taught us how to access the entire history of the universe throughout the whole of existence. No one could retain that much information, but we were trusted with the ship's vast computer system, so it was all at our fingertips. We now had the knowledge to travel anywhere in the universe, during any time—past, present, or future.

As I said, Ratchakokov was gracious, but naïve and a poor judge of character. He failed to detect Desi's ruthless ambition and my pathological need for bedlam. After two years honing our craft as intergalactic pirates, Desi and I staged our second mutiny.

After taking command of the Groaza, one of the adjustments we needed to make was in the manner of punishment. It was only a matter of time before some of the crew misbehaved. They were, after all, pirates. Captain Trevor had taught us back on the Horrendous, the first rule for maintaining obedience on a pirate ship, was to communicate to the crew that malefactors would be dealt with severely. Of all the punishments in the pirate handbook, there was only one penalty—death. We were left to our imaginations as to how to affect that. As sea pirates, having someone walk the plank was a straightforward thing. You just marched them at sword point off the edge of the ship. In space at hyper-speed, that was a difficult proposition. Desi found an alternative.

"We'll just stuff him into the garbage chute and shoot him into space," she suggested.

"Brilliant!" I agreed.

That was the last the ship ever saw of former Captain Ivan Ratchakokov.

As we spent the next four hundred years in real-time shuttling about the universe throughout the totality of existence, we discovered a few things. Some beneficial, like time travel halting the aging process. Desi and I were still in our mid-twenties four centuries later.

"Do you think we're immortal?" I asked.

"No," she said. "Ratchakokov surely died at our hands, and we lose a few men every raid. So, I think we can be killed. We just don't get older."

"Best we don't get careless then," I said.

Another happy discovery was that not only could we travel anywhere in the universe at any time, but we could return as many times as we saw fit. This was a good thing for the purse. The richest pirate prize ever taken in the whole breadth and history of the universe was the Urca de Lima, a Spanish galleon treasure ship taken and sunk off the coast of Florida, on planet Earth, in 1715. Gold being dearly valued everywhere in the universe, the gold lifted from that ship was worth more than two hundred million British Pounds in its contemporary time. The value in the present and future is priceless. Desi and I have taken it over a hundred times.

As time went on—ad infinitim—we received the inevitable challenges from disillusioned crew members who thought they were better suited to lead than Desi and *meself*. We thwarted every challenge, but the problem of the punishment serving as a deterrent for future attempted coups was a thorny one. In the old days on Earth, a simple keelhauling would suffice to dissuade further misguided ambitions. Witnessing the gory, painful, and slow death of a traitor being dragged across the barnacles on the bottom of the ship, tearing them to shreds while simultaneously drowning, would squelch even the most ambitious future treason. Keelhauling someone under a spaceship was an impractical matter, if not an impossibility. Desi, ever the creative one, hit on a solution.

"We'll find a planet with a craggy mountain range," she said. "Then we hover over the mountains and slowly drag the wretch until there's nothing left of him but his foot in the tractor beam."

"That would work," I nodded.

"Or," she said excitedly, "we'll find a planet with oceans that have sharks and sea monsters. We dangle the villain until just his head is above the water and wait for the sea beasties to have at him."

"That'll be enough, Desi," I said, wincing. "*Jaysus*, woman, but you scare me sometimes."

Thanks to Desdemona's diabolic planning and my swift and brutal execution, it would come as no surprise when we became the most feared pirates in universal history. But, in point of fact, only I did. Desi killed as many as I, but I got all the credit. Because she was a woman—and a beautiful one at that—no one believed she was capable of the carnage she committed. So, Captain Black Malachy O'Callaghan alone became the most wanted pirate in the universe. The fair Desdemona Kelly was believed to be my prisoner. If I weren't already the most sought-after fugitive in all of creation, imagine the innumerable conscripts attracted to the cause of a helpless damsel needing rescue from a cutthroat scoundrel like *meself*. It seems sexism isn't just timeless; it's eternal. What *bollocks!*

Our attempts to evade capture by the Crown Forces are what brought us to Casai Shima. Hoping to enjoy our spoils in a brief respite from raiding, Desi and I were holed up in a seaside bungalow. Lost in the throes of our unquenchable desire, the King's men came bursting through the door. They snatched me up in my altogether and thrashed me properly. Strangely, they set not a finger on Desi.

"Is this the infamous pirate, Malachy O'Callaghan?" the Crown's captain asked her.

She nodded, pulling the bedclothes tighter around her.

"You're a prisoner no more, Madam. You are safe now."

"Thank you," Desi said, weeping. "You can't imagine the hell of it all."

I couldn't believe she had betrayed me. She had picked this destination. Did she do so knowing the Crown's forces would be lying in wait for me? Had she arranged for them to be here? As bitter as the idea was, I bought into it. Upon interrogation, I lied and said she had always been my prisoner. I copped to every one of our shared crimes, exonerating her for all of them. There was no saving myself, but I couldn't bear the thought of her swinging from the gallows beside me. So, I would hang for us both.

As the hangman approached me unseen from the rear, the familiar scent of warm soda bread filled my nostrils. I felt gentle hands place the rough hemp rope over my head. I thought it peculiar there was no black hood. I wondered why, as it was customary to hood the condemned. Nothing seemed to be making sense at the moment. The noose was tightened *above* my Adam's apple, not below it, as it should have been. The knot was placed directly behind my head instead of behind the right ear. *This is all wrong*, I thought. *The rope is set too high on my throat. With the knot where it is, the fall won't snap my neck. I'll dangle here for hours, slowly strangling. Am I so detestable as to deserve this*

fate? This is what was running through my mind, until I heard the sweet voice of my beloved Desdemona whisper in my ear.

"When that rope gives way where I cut it, love, run straight over the bluffs in front of us," she said, undoing the bonds on my wrists. "At this point, it's only twelve feet down to the beach. Head for the shore. There is a zodiac with an outboard motor waiting for us there. The crew has the Groaza four hundred yards offshore, just under the surface, awaiting our arrival."

"Where shall we go?" I asked.

"The universe and all of time is your oyster," she said.

"I'm afraid you'll have to decide, my love. I'm a bit preoccupied at the moment."

"There is a Spanish galleon full of gold off the coast of Florida on planet Earth in the year 1715," she said, giggling. "I think we should take it again."

I was grinning broadly at the captain of the Crown's Forces when I heard the lever pulled and the floor disappear beneath my feet. As I dropped through the aperture of the gallows, I heard the sweet and satisfying sound of a rope snapping in two.

DEADLY VOYAGE

SUZANNE BAGINSKIE

One long blast and three shorts signaled the *Illumination of the Seas* cruise ship leaving the port of Nassau. High waves slapped the hull as we sailed deeper into the Atlantic Ocean. I stood on Deck Seventeen peering down at Deck Nine's open-air pool.

Caribbean Reggae music boomed through loudspeakers with cruisers bopping to the catchy rhythm. Vacationers attending the Bon Voyage-Sail Away party purchased beers and cocktails from smiling bar waiters. All three thousand-plus passengers traveling for the seven-day cruise had safely reembarked.

None of the revelers knew a man had been murdered eight floors up on Deck Seventeen.

It had all happened so quickly. Fifteen minutes earlier, I'd changed into shorts and a t-shirt, and slid my size elevens into Crocs. After grabbing my book, I headed for the nearby staircase and climbed two flights to floor seventeen.

I arrived on the portside deck around 6:10 p.m. Most early diners were seated at their assigned tables in the main restaurant making this a quiet reading spot. Situated near the stern, lots of cruisers avoided the rear aft of the ship. Nine of the ten complimentary chaise lounges sat empty. One passenger lay stretched out asleep about eight seats away covered by a beach blanket. I settled into a chaise and located the bookmarked page in my crime novel.

Juan, the bar waiter approached. "Need a drink, Ray?" About twenty, his left hand balanced a tray of curvy cocktail glasses and two beers.

"Why not. Bring me the usual, Corona." I passed him my set-sail card and he hurried off. Faint chimes dinged, and the alcove elevator doors slid open. I soon heard a female voice.

"Wake up, Glenn. Come on. You have to shower and dress for dinner."

Glancing over, I watched the thirty-something platinum-haired woman shake the sleeping man. Slightly plump like most other tourists, she probably visited the self-serving buffet line too often.

"Glenn. Wake up. Don't you hear me?" Her voice rose an octave and she tugged at the light blanket.

That's when I noticed several of the ship's beach towels had been wrapped tightly around her husband's stomach area and were soaked with his crimson-colored blood. She dropped the coverlet and screamed loudly.

"Help. Somebody, help me."

Tossing my book, I'd leaped from the chaise lounge, and rushed to her side. His sightless eyes stared at the deck's overhang. One by one, I unwound the beach towels, and discovered a gaping cavity in his lower abdomen. Puddles of blood lay beneath his chair on the varnished, wooden deck.

"Are you, his wife?"

"Yes, I'm Barbara Lewis." She sobbed and gazed at her husband. "My God, what happened to him?" She gagged.

"Not sure, but he's gone, Mrs. Lewis." I scanned our surroundings. Three empty beer bottles and an ashtray holding mashed cigarettes sat on a small patio table next to him. Only suite owners had permission to smoke here. One butt had reddish lip imprints. When I glanced back at the woman, tears gushed like a waterfall down her cheeks, but she wore no trace of lipstick.

Footsteps neared. I turned and saw the waiter holding my beer. His hazel eyes narrowed when he focused on the man and bloody mess. He froze, as if a statue.

I'd patted his back. "Juan. Alert the crew. It's a medical emergency."

He grabbed his radio and announced over the P.A. system interrupting the Reggae music, "Code Alpha, Deck 17 Aft, Stern area." A hush rose below. He repeated it a second time. The man's wife collapsed into a chair, weeping.

So much for being alone and relaxing with my book. This had turned into a deadly voyage and was the last thing I'd wanted to get involved in. I'd either be classified as a witness or a suspect or even accused of murdering the poor man.

While I'd waited for help, I'd stared below the railing watching all those travelers drinking, dancing, and enjoying their lives, unknowing how easily death came calling.

Within six minutes, Dr. Lorenzo, and two men juggling a stretcher arrived. The doctor, hired about three months ago, had lots of experience. I'd heard his qualifications beat out many other applicants. Following behind them, the Chief Security Officer, Ivan Vecchio and Olaf, his deputy.

Vecchio stood six feet tall and had the blackest eyes I'd ever seen. Originally from Italy, he wore a name badge pinned to his official white uniform and two security patches on his shoulders. Responsible for maintaining safety and passenger control, he also supervised the Security Guards who policed points of entry at the gangway gates and tender docking stations.

Dr. Lorenzo immediately kneeled beside the chaise and took the man's vitals. He looked over at Vecchio and shook his head. "This man has had surgery. I'm guessing his kidneys are missing, and with the loss of all that blood, no way he'd survive. Surely it wasn't done here on this chair?"

Vecchio studied the scene. "I'm not believing this. Last month someone fell overboard. We never found him. Now this." He grimaced and turned to his deputy. "Olaf, as soon as possible please have Deck Seventeen cordoned off and post no entry signs. Get word to the crew to be on the lookout for an area that may have been used for an operation and any sign of blood."

"Yes, sir." Deputy Olaf headed into the elevator area.

"Do we know who this is?" Vecchio asked and looked at the woman.

Barbara Lewis sniffled and said, "He's my husband, Glenn. I came to wake him for dinner." Her voice cracked. "We were supposed to celebrate our tenth anniversary tonight," she sobbed and hugged herself.

Vecchio eyed me next.

"When I first arrived, I thought he was just sleeping. So, I slipped into a chaise and opened my book. Juan came and I ordered a beer."

Juan nodded.

Vecchio turned to the medical crew. "I need to take some pictures and fingerprints, and then you can transport the body to the morgue. Dr. Lorenzo, please follow them and start your incident paperwork."

"Should the scene be disturbed so soon?" I asked.

"We're in territorial waters and Maritime Law gives the FBI jurisdiction over crimes committed on cruise ships. I'll start the process by collecting evidence and getting the facts recorded for the authorities. They'll come aboard and take control of the case when we dock in the port of Cancun."

I wasn't familiar with law at sea. His answer made sense.

Not long after, they lifted the body onto a stretcher and covered it with a white sheet. The staff members headed straight toward a crew elevator.

Vecchio said, "I want each of you to briefly tell me what happened."

Glenn's wife, Barbra Lewis, went first. "My husband and I remained onboard at the port. After lunch around 1:00 p.m., we went to the casino." She wiped away tears. "He played a few hands of Blackjack, but Lady Luck didn't favor him. He lost his daily quota quickly. Glenn found me at my usual slot machine and told me he would return to our room, change into his swimsuit and later, take a nap on Deck Seventeen."

Vecchio listened and jotted notes on his phone.

Juan and I didn't have very much to add.

"I'll need to take a signed statement from each of you in my office. One at a time, of course. Please follow me."

I knew about interviewing witnesses. I asked myself, how many times had I interrogated suspects?

For thirty-eight years, I'd worked as an undercover detective rubbing elbows with the nastiest people on earth. After losing my wife to cancer, I hung on with the Atlanta Police Force until I reached sixty-five, so I could earn the maximum pension.

After dealing with dangerous criminals and gang members, who'd recognize me if I'd stayed local, I made a life changing decision. I'd bought an Owner's Suite package on the *Illumination of the Seas* cruise ship docked at Port Canaveral, Florida. Located on Deck Fifteen, the stateroom had its own balcony, offered round the clock meals, house-keeping, and entertainment. I loved my nautical home.

Hidden away in my roomy cabin for over a year and a half now, I'd sailed the bluest ocean, slept like a baby on a king-sized bed, and enjoyed the sights. Not to mention the food. I used my new WitSec identity name, Ray Anderson from Georgia. My fake background included managing Radio Systems, Inc, a company that sold two-way radios, scanners, and cell phone equipment. Before I boarded, I grew a beard and mustache and shaved off my hair. Life was great. Until now. No one on the boat had a clue about my past. And that's the way I wanted it to stay.

Most of the crew knew me as Ray, especially Vecchio, the Security Chief. We'd become good friends. After he took my statement, Juan, the bar waiter gave his next. He'd verified my many afternoons spent on Deck Seventeen, reading. Should I be worried? Could that have been me? An alternative theory nagged inside my head. Has someone from my past been seeking revenge, or discovered my whereabouts? When Vecchio's questioning finally ended, I breathed a sigh of relief. I'd be looking over my shoulder till he solved the crime. For now, I'd rather be safely in my cabin.

I hurried down one flight and stopped on the next floor landing. Ying Lee, my cabin steward, and his helper Anton stood conversing with a pretty brunette about twenty-five. I paused and greeted them.

"This is Dora Benito from Spain. She's new. Anton's teaching her how to clean cabins," Ying Lee said. "Dora, this is Ray Anderson. His cabin is on Deck Fifteen." She smiled.

"Welcome aboard, Miss Dora." I stared into gorgeous brown eyes enhanced by flawless olive skin. Her full pouty lips, natural or collagen were ripe for kissing. She'd look more like a dancer who'd perform on the ship's stage. Her beauty would be wasted cleaning cabins. "Nice to meet you." She blushed and lowered her eyes. The three stayed on that level and I continued to mine. I hiked to my cabin and tapped my set-sail card key against the door slot.

Upon entering, the terrace curtains fluttered in the evening breeze. I grit my teeth. I hadn't left the balcony door open.

Someone had been in my stateroom.

I crept into the separate bedroom and bath, both were empty. So was the balcony. I slid the glass door shut and locked it. Then hurried to a small cabinet that housed a miniature safe holding all my important documents, passport, and jewelry. Only I had the code. Nothing inside was disturbed.

I scanned the closet nook. My black tuxedo jacket sleeve stuck out of a garment bag in the opened wardrobe. I hadn't worn the black-tie outfit since Elegant Night, about a week ago. The pants had really pinched my waistline. The following morning, I'd committed myself to walking three miles on the treadmill every day in the spa's fitness center.

My hands trembled. The WitSec counselor had warned me there'd be close calls like this and not to get spooked.

So, who had opened it?

Perhaps my cabin steward, Ying Lee, had checked my closet for laundry. The bed was turned down for the night, and fresh towels hung in the bathroom. I shrugged, tucked the dinner jacket in and rezipped the bag. Quite confident, Ying Lee wouldn't have left the balcony door open. He'd been assigned to my room since day one.

One thing I knew for certain, I'd always closed my closet and sliding glass doors. With the ship's constant movement, I'd been briefed that all rooms were designed with locking features in case of rough seas or hurricanes. Someone else had entered my room. What were they looking for?

~

The next morning, I sat alone in the Lido Buffet Deck near a huge window. Today's itinerary scheduled a full sail day and as far as I could see we were surrounded by dark gray clouds and navy-blue waves with no land in sight. Security Chief Vecchio entered the seating area and headed my way with his breakfast tray. "Do you mind if I join you?"

"Not at all." This wasn't unusual. We spoke often. He'd sensed my knowledge of policing, which I explained was from selling equipment to county Sheriff's Offices and Police Departments for thirty years. They not only purchased my company's police radio, scanners, and handheld transmitters, at times they brought me cell phones to trace for evidence dealing with crimes. That's what I told him anyway. "Any news on yesterday's murder?"

His dark eyes narrowed to slits. "In one of the crew's working areas, we found a steel table used for folding freshly washed towels and sheets with blood spots on the leg. I took samples and photographed the scene. In theory, I believe the murderers planned on pushing his body overboard to the sharks after the operation. Until they heard your footsteps on the stairs."

"That makes sense, who'd be the wiser."

"Ray, do you know what harvesting is?"

"Sorry to say, I do. People have been well-known to remove kidneys and resell them for a hefty price. That takes planning."

He looked away. "I can't wrap my head around how someone got off the ship with human organs."

"Do they allow cruisers to bring coolers on the ship? Whoever did this would need an organ preservation storage and some dry ice." I stared at him and hoped I hadn't said too much.

"Yes, but only twelve-by-twelve containers."

"I saw a medical documentary once showing a skilled surgeon actively doing a kidney transplant. It took three hours to remove the organ from the donor. Glenn's wife last saw him in the casino at 1:30 p.m., before he headed to their room."

"We found him much later. Plenty of time for the surgery, they didn't care if he lived."

The thought chilled me. I never had an organ harvesting case, but I had worked drug cases and prostitution and met with the FBI handling Human Trafficking once or twice. I'd heard the FBI say Organ Trafficking crimes were booming globally in the twenty-first century. Just not on cruise ships.

"You may be looking for two or three perps. A recruiter who seeks out an unknown victim, and another who sells and transports the organs. Then there's the unscrupulous medical practitioner who drugs the person and performs the transplant. They are listed as the most immoral con artists in today's world."

Vecchio studied my face. "How do you know all this?" He smiled.

"I read a lot of mysteries and watch thriller movies." My answer seemed to satisfy him.

"Captain Falcone didn't take this very well. We're both worried about the ship's safety rating. It effect's our pay raises, too. He's quite strict and read me the riot act. I don't know how to turn this around, except to find the murderer before we reach land. That would please the Captain."

"I've spoken with him once or twice. He welcomed me aboard when I signed the residential contract. I get the impression he keeps to himself."

"He does. I know he likes to drink and surround himself with females. When they invite passengers to the Captain's dinner, he always picks out the most attractive women. They fuss over him because of his status. Remember he's Italian like me. We love the ladies." Vecchio rose, deposited his tray at the service station and left.

He didn't know, before I signed my contract to purchase the cabin, I thoroughly looked into all the officers, the company's reputation, and other vital information. With my security clearance, I could view confidential documents on file. Everyone had a favorable past, except Captain Falcone. One black mark tarnished his bio.

At the age of seventeen, authorities arrested him as a supporter of the Italian Mafia faction in Rome. The members consisted of crooked businessmen, politicians, and officials, all led by a former far-right terrorist. The group had been active in the capital for the better part of ten years, skimming hundreds of millions of euros. A few members testified under oath Falcone wasn't involved at all, but in the right place at the wrong time. His attorney cleared him of any wrongdoing. I decided to believe the testimony. Since he became a captain twenty years ago, his reputation rate rose favorably, and he'd been praised several times.

After breakfast, I returned to my cabin and found Ying Lee vacuuming. When I walked in, he switched off his machine. "I'll be done soon, Mr. Ray." Petite and thin, he had thirty-five cabins to clean each day. I marveled at how he remembered all the cruiser's names and also when he'd have access to service their units.

"No hurry. I just need to brush my teeth and then I am attending a session on acupuncture." I went into the bathroom and remembered I wanted to ask him about last night. He'd finished before I came out and left a towel monkey hanging near the balcony door. I grinned.

I headed for the comedy club where they were holding the acupuncture session and slid into a seat near the stage.

"Ladies and gentlemen. I want to introduce Dr. Seng to you. He is originally from Beijing, China," the cruise staffer said. He read Dr. Seng's bio stating he was a licensed M.D. and surgeon in the U.S. Everyone clapped.

The word surgeon stood out. He must have boarded yesterday. I'd give his name to Vecchio later. Have I ever seen Dr. Seng? Short and stout, his bald head shone beneath the stage lights. I've met many different people and crew members since I arrived. Cruise ships advertised jobs constantly and attracted new crew members from all nations.

Doctor Seng gave a little history about the discovery of acupuncture. He projected charts on the screen and explained how inserting five needles into certain body points would provide pain relief for arthritis, migraines, and other medical problems. The attendees, mostly retirement-aged travelers, who had the time and savings to take long trips, asked a lot of questions. He ended by displaying a clipboard with an appointment list for cruisers who wanted to meet with him and discuss their issues. For a hefty fee of course.

My left knee pained me occasionally, but I knew acupuncture wasn't the answer. Dr. Seng emphasized he'd be onboard for two days till our next stop if anyone who hadn't signed up changed their mind. When the ship docked in Cancun, he'd debark and reboard another ship to hold his program all over again. Very profitable for both him and the cruise ships.

When I first settled in my cabin, I'd chosen the 8:00 p.m. dinner seating and the later theater shows. As a resident they gave me reserved theater seating right in the center, four rows back from the stage. Tonight's show had a comic ventriloquist. He lifted a TSA Security Agent puppet from his lap and told him to glance at the audience. Then asked him where they were. The puppet's eyes roamed the lower theater and then the balcony. He turned to the entertainer and said, "Are we in a nursing home?" The crowd roared.

Cabin stewards, Anton and Dora were right in the seats in front of me. Could they be sweet on each other already? His arm slid around her shoulders. I'd seen a couple of shipboard romances. They usually fizzled out. Intermission arrived and these two started whispering. I heard her say she didn't like the show.

"We have to stay, it would be rude to leave, Dora," Anton answered. She pouted those red lips and made a face. "You need to remain calm, let me order you a drink when the bar waiter comes. Doc said you did an excellent job flirting the other afternoon. In two days, you'll leave the ship and find another job on land."

Hmm. Maybe she changed her mind about a nine-month stint of making beds, cleaning toilets and catering to the public. A job on a cruise ship wasn't for everyone. The ventriloquist returned and finished within a half hour. I stifled a yawn on the way to my cabin. In the morning, I had a 7:00 a.m. appointment with a treadmill.

I walked inside my suite and pulled at my tie. Somebody coughed.

I took a few steps and peered into the bedroom. A strange man stood there. "Why are you in my cabin? Get out."

I guess I scared him. He raced toward the door. I backed up and blocked it. He turned and started toward the balcony, but that meant jumping off the ship. He stopped in his tracks.

"Sir. I'm Joshua. I'm replacing Ying Lee for service in your room this evening." Tall and muscular for a steward, and not wearing a uniform, he had to be an American. His wavy bleached hair flipped to one side. The other had been closely shaven. He looked like he sang in a rock band. Though, I'd never seen him perform on our stage.

"Who are you really? What happened to Ying Lee?"

"He wasn't feeling well and went to sick bay. I'm his replacement. I hung new towels in your bathroom. Go check."

I peered in. They were hanging neatly, and the toilet paper was creased with their signature "V". "Joshua, you can leave now. I'll turn down the bed cover myself."

"Thank you, sir. I'll be back in the morning." He hurried around me and fled from the room.

I secured the inner door lock. What had happened to Ying Lee?

The next morning, I rose and tugged back my balcony curtain. I saw the shoreline. We were due to arrive in Cancun the next day. Had the ship arrived earlier than scheduled? The ocean remained calm and flat. No engines vibrated beneath my feet. We were anchored.

The room speaker came on air. "This is the Captain speaking. We have a medical emergency aboard our ship and we are seeking help from the local hospital on the island of Puerto Rico. There's no reason to panic. We hope to be on our way soon. Check out your flier for the planned daily activities. I'll make another announcement when we're ready to leave port."

I picked up the room phone that tied into their system and dialed sick bay. "This is Ray Anderson calling from Cabin 219. Would you please tell me if Ying Lee is still in there?"

"Hey, Ray. It's Mary. I'm afraid Ying Lee's condition has worsened.

We are administering fluids and making him and the others comfortable."

"How many patients do you have?"

"Six crew members and five cruisers. The ship can't handle too many more. Dr. Lorenzo is tendering over to the island for some help from their medical facility."

"Thanks, Mary." I replaced the receiver.

I needed more information. I left my cabin, took an elevator to the upper deck restaurant and searched for a senior security officer I might know. They'd usually had firsthand knowledge of the ship's happenings. I spotted Deputy Olaf sitting alone sipping coffee. I approached.

"Good morning, Ray. Is there something I can help you with?"

"Yes, there is. What's going on in the Infirmary? My steward's in there sick and he isn't the only one."

"I've heard a few people have a stomach virus, and they are giving them fluids."

"Mary told me it's spreading. Is it Norovirus? There hasn't been a breakout since I've boarded."

"Shh. Please keep it to yourself, Ray. Vecchio is waiting for Dr. Lorenzo to tender over to Puerto Rico for information about the Norovirus within the next few hours. We may have to quarantine people in their cabins. Please don't discuss this with anyone else. I only told you since you're a legal resident on this ship. The crew's been instructed to keep the passenger's calm. They are also monitoring anyone who looks sick."

I returned to my cabin and watched a mystery movie to take my mind off things. I decided to search for a new reading spot after lunch. Deck Seventeen was still off limits. I ate a bowl of hot soup in the Lido Buffet, and then hiked the stairs to the fitness level. All five chaise lounges were empty. I sat and concentrated on my book.

A Spanish accent reached my ears. Dora Benito walked out on the fitness deck chatting on her iPhone. She wore a pearly-white bikini that didn't leave much to the imagination. She settled into an empty chair and opened a laptop computer. I slid on sunglasses and watched her every move. Five minutes later, her cell phone played La Bomba. She grabbed it, slid the computer off her lap and slipped out of sight into the nearby corridor.

I leaped from the chaise and went over to peek at her monitor's screen. Passenger names were listed with room numbers. Footsteps sounded. I raced to my chair and picked up my book like I was leaving. In the alcove, I pressed for an elevator, but when it arrived, I let the door close and hid in another corridor.

Pretty soon, Dora came in and sped down the stairs. I crept slowly behind her. She seemed to be searching room numbers on Deck Sixteen. I followed. When she stopped at Cabin 643, she knocked and leaned her computer bag against the outer wall.

The door opened. She forced her way in. The door shut and locked. I neared and heard arguing inside. A steward approached me. "Hey," I said. I forgot my key, can you open it please." I wiggled the door handle. He smiled, stuck in his master key and the lock clicked. I held the door ajar. He kept on walking by. Once he cleared the hallway, I entered.

Dora had Glenn's wife pressed against the balcony rail. She screamed at her in Spanish.

I yelled, "Hey, what are you doing?" I rushed to them before Dora could push Barbara overboard and grabbed Dora's wrists, freeing Barbara. She ran to the makeshift desk.

"Dial security. Now," I ordered. Dora struggled, but I wouldn't let her go. For many years, I'd carried handcuffs in my back pocket. Not anymore. Too bad. She cursed me in Spanish, then bit my upper arm. I pulled her head away and saw red teeth mark impressions.

"Barbara, do you know her?"

"Not really. She was assigned at our dinner table with a guy named Joshua and sat next to my Glenn. I didn't like how she flirted with him. Two nights ago, she begged him to dance with her. The crew doned ruffled-sleeved costumes and encouraged passengers to dance with them to that Macarena Latin song. Glenn had a few too many. He took her up on it. Afterward, I told her off in front of the other diners at the table and embarrassed her. She hollered something in Spanish as we left."

I looked at both women. Why would Dora want to toss Barbara over the balcony? Maybe she held a grudge from the other evening.

Someone knocked hard on the door. Deputy Olaf had arrived. He had a weird look on his face.

"Hold on. I can explain everything." But could I?

After Deputy Olaf took Dora below, I returned to my room and waited for Vecchio to contact me for a statement on this new incident. He wanted to question Dora first and then Joshua. Forty-five minutes later, he was ready.

As I traveled there, Captain Falcone's voice rang out loud and clear.

"This is the captain speaking and I have some good news. We will be sailing again in thirty minutes to the port of Cancun. Weather is sunny and hot there, with a temperature of 29 Celsius or 85 degrees in U.S. terms. The seas are calm, and no storms are on the horizon. It should be smooth sailing all night. I expect to arrive at 8:00 a.m. and debarkation at the port will begin an hour later. Have a good afternoon and evening."

I arrived, knocked, and entered Vecchio's office. "Please sit down, Ray." I settled into a chair facing him. He looked stern and downright pissed. I shifted in my seat.

"I have interrogated Ms. Dora Benito, also known as Dora Lorenzo and her associate Joshua Bennett."

"Lorenzo. Is she related to Dr. Lorenzo onboard?"

"She's his daughter. He helped her and Joshua get false passports. She's married to Joshua Bennett. The pair came onboard to apply for jobs as stewards, but they had other plans."

"She's really pretty, I couldn't believe she'd wanted to be a cabin steward?"

"Precisely. It was all a ruse. Remember you told me there's usually two or three perpetrators that steal organs?"

"I do." What was he about to tell me?

Someone rapped on the door.

"Come in," Vecchio said.

Deputy Olaf entered carrying a black bag. "They told the truth, chief. I found it right where they said it would be. I'll see you later." He set the bag on the desk between us.

I stiffened. What was going on here?

Vecchio stuck his fingers into green rubber gloves and opened the bag.

"Check out this fancy leather medical bag." He reached inside. "Here's a surgeon's scalpel." He held it up to the light. "Hmm, it has a hint of blood on it." Next, he pulled out surgical clips, wiping gauge, prepackaged needles, and drug bottles. "There's even an unopened spool of suture thread and a pack of sewing needles."

"Is that blood from Glenn Lewis?"

"I'm sure we will find it matches his."

"So, what are you getting at? Was Dora and Joshua in league with Dr. Lorenzo, the surgeon, and were they all involved with stealing those two kidneys?"

"Yes. Harvesting organs pays much better than cruise ships. By the way, that unscheduled stop today in Puerto Rico was not to check out our twenty-four-hour virus. There's no Norovirus aboard. Turns out Dr. Lorenzo was taking an organ preservation storage container with him to the medical facility. Those kidneys were being sold to an unknown man for a hefty $50,000 price. Just like you told me, kidneys can survive thirty-six to forty-eight hours, if kept on dry ice."

"How did you find out?"

"One of my security guys at the docking station saw the box tucked away beneath a tender seat. Afraid it would slide, he moved it. Then he realized it hadn't been properly logged out. He called me and I told him to cut it open. He got quite a surprise. I instructed him not to let the vessel leave. When I arrived, Dr. Lorenzo had a smug look on his face. I immediately arrested him. He's in our jail. So is his daughter and Joshua Bennett."

"This is like one of those high crimes thriller novels I read, but I never saw any plot like

this happening on a cruise ship."

He grinned. "When we land in Cancun, the FBI will come aboard and I can turn them all over, along with my files. Thanks for your help along the way." He grinned. "Incidentally, one more thing. They stashed this medical bag in your wardrobe closet. I guess you don't dress in that suit too much."

"My closet. Why me?"

"The three of them confessed. When they heard you approach, they dumped Mr. Lewis in the chaise lounge instead of tossing him over-board to the sharks. Then waited undercover to see who arrived. While I questioned you, they must have borrowed Ying Lee's master key without his knowledge and went into your cabin. They slipped the bag beneath everything hanging inside your closet. Most likely to throw suspicion on you after they left the ship. After all, you were the first person who entered the deck, before his wife discovered him dead."

"Wow. Thanks for that information."

He didn't know those same thoughts ran through my mind when the wife found her husband. Someone had been in my room, afterall. Now that the case was solved, there's no need to keep looking over my shoulder.

MEETUP IN THE BERMUDA TRIANGLE

JIM TRITTEN

The thing about flying at night, at sea, with no moon or stars, is there is no horizon. No way to distinguish where the air ends and the water begins. You have to trust your instruments. Your guideposts are the artificial horizon, attitude gyro, and vertical speed indicators.

That night, a chilly day in December, was very dark. Flashes from the towering thunderstorm ahead provided the only lights. And, of course, the white and cobalt blue flames coming out of the exhaust stacks on either side of the A-1E's massive Wright 2700 horsepower engine and the red and green wingtip lights. This old bird had been designed before I was born and had the looks of a classic World War II fighter.

The rule about thunderstorms is to fly as low as possible underneath the severe weather. I decided five hundred feet was about right. Enough altitude to live through a sudden downdraft. High enough to be well over the tiny Caribbean atolls and keys that dot the Bahama Islands. The steady drone of the engine lulled me into a fixation on the artificial horizon, and I neglected to watch whether I was holding my altitude or on a slow descent.

The warning button on the radar altimeter turned red, and an audible alarm sounded in my helmet's earphones. I shook my head, blinked, and pulled back on the stick while I added about ten inches of engine manifold pressure to permit me to gain altitude and level off again at five hundred feet. I throttled back to cruise settings and double-checked my heading against the magnetic wet compass. I was three hundred fifty miles off the coast. There is no chance I would miss hitting the United States but not sure I would be anywhere near the St. John's River exit to the open ocean. This area of the Caribbean had been labeled the Bermuda Triangle for numerous strange occurrences, including navigation difficulties. Then too, there was that story about the missing Flight Nineteen – five Fort Lauderdale-based Navy TBM Avenger torpedo planes disappearing over these same waters in December 1945.

As I passed under the thunderstorms, the windscreen lit up with electrical sparks that crawled from the center outward. I glanced out to the wings and saw the St. Elmo's Fire advance from the fuselage outboard to each wingtip. I watched the meteorological phenomenon, and it didn't seem to affect the navigation lights or my instruments.

Not much to do as I motored along and passed through the bad weather. I flipped the toggle switch to see if I could pick up the automatic direction-finding radio beacon on New Providence Island. The number one needle swung from side to side, pointing back to the thunderstorms. *No sense trying to use the onboard navigation aids. Just keep flying west, report back to the ship "feet dry" when I was over land. Then figure out if I was north or south of the St. John's River. From that point, it'd be a cakewalk to follow the eastern shore to the welcoming white and green rotating beacon at the Mayport Naval Air Station.*

The audible alarm from the radar altimeter woke me up, and I instinctively pulled back on the stick and added throttle. The aircraft responded, and the altitude warning alert ceased. I again shook my head and thought how lucky I was to have technology work in my favor. I reduced power and stretched my torso and legs – time to dig out the maps.

The windscreen filled with an opaque gray, and I realized I had entered a fog bank. *Focus on the attitude gyro, keep the wings level, and maintain altitude.*

I reached down to the documents pouch on the right side of the cockpit. I extracted the aviation charts for the southeast U.S. As I turned my head back up to the left, I had difficulty getting my eyeballs to steady on the artificial horizon. My stomach churned with foul-smelling burps escaping my gut. My head hurt – classic symptoms of vertigo or spatial disorientation.

Focus on the attitude gyro. Ignore what my body is telling me. I am not in a turn to the left and a climb. The artificial horizon shows wings level. Do not touch the stick. Disregard the pain in my head. Keep my head steady and don't move it to further upset the semi-circular canals in my ears. The sloshing of fluids will settle down if I can sit still.

My nausea intensified, and I opened my helmet bag just in case I needed to barf.

I knew I was in a turn, and the instruments were wrong. I turned to the right and took off power to compensate. *There, that feels better. I'll have this bird thoroughly checked before taking it back to the aircraft carrier.*

The feel of the plane seemed normal. I smiled without a care in the world as the A-1E struck the water, cartwheeled, and came to a stop amid the screeches and sounds of tearing metal.

It was daylight when my eyes opened, and I stood outside the cockpit on a sandy treeless island. My A-1E sat upright on a windswept beach. Somehow it was resting on its landing gear, and there was no damage to the airframe. I patted my body to see if I could feel my touch, and everything felt the way it should. I removed my helmet and orange Mae West and dropped them on the sand.

"Hi there." A voice came from behind me.

I turned to face the source. I saw five young naval aviators in World War II-era tan flight suits and cloth headgear. Five TBM Avengers sat on their landing gear undamaged. On the side of each aircraft was stenciled, NAS Ft. Lauderdale. It looked just like the flyers that appeared at the ending of the movie *Close Encounters of the Third Kind.*

The Bermuda Triangle is real?

One of the other flyers shouted and asked, "What year are you from?"

LOVE OF THE BLACK LADY

R. J. ERBACHER

Allen was standing on the hotel balcony as the sun set over the water turning the skyline into a vibrant orange tableau. A painting that could have been on a wall in MOMA or a photograph in a Soho gallery. But he wasn't home in Manhattan tonight, but a small sibling of the Virgin Islands, listening to the waves splashing on the shore in the distance. They sounded like soft whispers calling him, inviting him because they knew this was his final night.

A dinner was in order, a last meal. Food was probably the only thing that didn't repulse him, and he was able to indulge without much consequences. Allen had a body that was lean and disease free. Cholesterol, blood pressure, heart rate all at their appropriate levels for a thirty-year-old male. He did very little in the form of exercise except for swimming; still he was able to maintain a respectable physique. At six foot-one with a calm face and a full head of dark brown hair you would think he would have no troubles attracting a girlfriend. A steady income kept him well-dressed and provided a comfortable apartment. Yet none of these attributes had promoted him to a sense of fulfillment. No children. No family. His parents were dead and he had no siblings. Any other relations were distant ones whom he had not known in a decade. Since high school he hadn't had friends. Business acquaintances never expanded beyond the workplace. He spent a great deal of his life in quiet solitude. That was actually what he needed back twelve years ago to cope with circumstances and now fate, or stubbornness, would not allow his persona to change.

The meal he ordered was adequate, and went to the bar afterwards and had a few glasses of VSOP. Sitting there sipping he watched couples dancing. They all looked as if they were happy, romantic partners enjoying their vacation. Enjoying each other. Enjoying life.

He had eaten alone and now he drank alone. If he could have pinpointed it, he supposed he unwittingly gave off an aura of required distance. Even a couple of single girls at a nearby table, who happen to be on holiday at the resort hoping to meet an interesting guy, were strangely compelled to avoid him. This shell of aloneness probably originated the summer after his graduation from Montpelier High School in Northern Ohio. Allen's mom and dad had been typically doting parents to an only child. His father was the foundation of the family providing abundant financial and inspirational support, happy to rearrange his work schedule so he could be at all his swimming events. His mom was content being the homemaker and caring for her husband and son. One little happy family.

Then his father developed brain cancer two months before the end of the school year and they kept it from him so he could make it through his last few swim meets and his finals without the burden of the news. Three weeks after he received his diploma his father was dead. His mom, unable to cope, killed herself less than a month later by taking an overdose. Prescribed for her so she could 'manage through this difficult time,' her solution was to check out of life, leaving Allen to handle the monumental burdens of his truncated family. Her suicide note contained the phrase 'I'm sorry' eleven times. Still battling the shock of his father's demise, Allen buried his mom on autopilot. Friends, his father's business associates, even the local priest tried counseling him after the double deaths but he shunned them all. He took a couple of months to settle the affairs, never leaving his house. When he was finished, he wanted nothing to do with his hometown or anybody he had known there. Allen sold the property and most of the valuables, took the proceeds and insurance money and moved to New York City. He enrolled in City College in the winter, bunked there without hardly acknowledging his roommate or making a single acquaintance in two years and unobtrusively managed an associate's degree in business. The college's placement program set him up in a job that he still worked at today. Since he left Montpelier, he hadn't had the energy or inclination to dwell on his past.

After downing the third glass of brandy he headed back to his suite, where he sat on the bed for a long time thinking but not registering, then undressed. The only thing he left was a twenty-dollar tip for the maid. He wasn't about to leave some sentimental note like his mom had, begging the world for forgiveness. There was nothing to be sorry about, no one to be sorry to.

Someone once said, "get busy living or get busy dying." For Allen there was no imaginable reason left to live. He made his choice.

His bare feet slapped on the tan stone slabs that guided guests toward the beach. His penis bounced from side to side as he walked in the long shadows of palm trees created by the few scattered spot lights around the complex. It was an hour past midnight and most of the couples were either in their rooms having sex or still out at the night-clubs and casinos. He passed only one pair hugging each other for support. The girl just giggled and half hid her face, pointing. The guy said "Right on. You go buddy," and they continued on their way nonplused. The beach was deserted. Once he was beyond the rough planked boardwalk there were no more lights and he had no further fear of being discovered. His toes flexed into the fine sand of the cool beach as he walked. Soon the pliable grains turned firm and he was standing on the edge of the earth, his feet playfully being caressed by the object of his desire. A healthy inhale filled him with the salty scent of the night. He stared into the darkness.

At this time yesterday he had been standing in this same place, fully clothed, the soft breeze gently tossing his hair, mesmerized by the sea's beauty. She was a vision in the night, all aglow with a silky pale sheen, compliments of the full moon and highlighted with a tapestry of a million tiny star fires. Oh, how much Allen wanted her at that moment. Easily he could understand the voluptuous attributes that sailors bestowed onto her, what they respectfully referred to as their 'lady.' For hours he stood there and watched until he could no longer rebuff her flirtations. He had to leave or he would have dove in head long right then and there, but like all momentous occasions he had planned the right time, the right mood.

Now was the time and just like a fickle lady she had changed dramatically. Heavy clouds blotted out the moon and stars, strong winds blew seawater mist in his face. A storm was brewing off in the distance someplace, out over the water where no one on earth would notice. Before him lay two black planes joined in a perfect line; the black sky meeting with the blacker ocean. No longer were the wave's whispers but heavy sighs of moistened breath, shamelessly luring him to come.

Slowly, he moved into the rippling curls. The water rose up his legs as he entered, touched his thighs, licked at his groin wetting his pubic hairs and made him erect, reacting as if a lover's hand had fondled him. He pushed forward submerging himself into the wetness, propelling through the opaque water. Floating easily to the surface, Allen began to swim.

Swimming was as instinctive as walking to him. He was a strong swimmer, always had been. Until he first tried out for the school swim team, Allen had no idea that his athletic prowess was an aquatic one. Mr. Hanraity, his science teacher and the swimming coach, told him he was a natural from the first time he plunged in and stroked across the length of the school pool as a lanky sophomore. In his senior year he won two division gold medals, setting a record time in his final meet and was being courted by a couple of college athletic scouts when his parents died and his world fell into the abyss. For nine years he didn't go near a pool and then finally one day he used the facility at the gym where his office provided free use of the exercise equipment as part of a new company employee good health program. It had been a long time and he instantly realized how much he missed swimming. He supposed the familiarity of the refreshing water was as close as he would come to connecting with an old friend. Now Allen worked out for an hour or so, three to four times a week at a posh Manhattan swim club and although many of the members and staff begged him to compete in organized meets, he politely refused, content to enjoy his solitary early morning laps. But when he arrived yesterday at this beautiful island resort, he shunned the luxurious pool. And other than that one stretch of admiration last night he'd stayed away from the ocean as well.

And now, at last, he was inside her, moving fluently with smooth even strokes, alternating the force of his body between each drive of an arm or leg. After a short while he started to feel the slight burn in his limbs that signaled the beginning of stress on his muscles.

Allen swam straight into the waves, heading for the reef that surrounded the cove of water in a semicircle around the resort. A quarter mile from the beach, the ocean's mighty waves would crash into the reef and deaden the impact of their force allowing just a cute little curl of water to unfold onto the golden sand. The small barrier reef, an ancient collection of the exoskeletons of countless generations of coral, rose up from the ocean floor and grew to just the level of the sea. From the shore it could be seen as a craggy ridge each time a wave broke on top of it and the ocean sank into the valley of the proceeding next wave. The unique combination allowed spectacular glimpses of the distant thundering tide while maintaining the peacefulness of the inner lagoon, gentle enough for the leisurely frolicking of resort guests.

Strangely enough he started to tire quickly and he wasn't quite sure why. He had only been swimming for ten minutes and he felt exhausted. Maybe his inactivity all day had worked against him, devaluing his muscles instead of preparing them. Usually, he could do half an hour without stopping. Allen always stretched out before entering the pool and he hadn't done that tonight and that was possibly having an adverse effect on him but after all did any of it matter? It wasn't as if he was worried about cramping and the drain on his system would actually be beneficial to his ultimate cause. At some point he would need to succumb to the fatigue. He could hear the phosphorus white caps breaking just ahead so he knew the first phase of his ordeal was near its close.

The discoloration of the reef could easily be seen in daylight separating the crystal blue of the inner, calmer water from the dense blue of the deeper ocean beyond and into infinity. Now it was just an invisible scar in a colorless sea. The noise pounded into the natural barrier like wet thunder and it roared into his ears. It became so overwhelmingly monotone that he didn't know he had reached the reef until he bumped his shoulder sharply against it. Allen found purchase and climbed up onto the living structure but unsteady footing left him with a wobbly balance, the spray of the diffused waves nearly knocking him over. He checked his shoulder in the darkness and felt the stickiness of an open gash. First blood had been drawn. She was in a malicious mood this evening.

Gasping as he crawled forward, not realizing how much the trek was going to take out of him, Allen scanned the surroundings. He hadn't ever remembered being outside when it was as black out as this night was. Turning back for a quick glance to the resort he saw only a line of lighted dots, the spotlights on the boardwalk that rimmed the beach looking like a string of ivory

Christmas bulbs in the distance. The ornamental horizon seemed as if it were a hazy dream. He had asked the proprietor of the surf shop, a Californian transplant, how far it was from the shore to the reef? "Just over a quarter mile, man," was his emphatic response. Looking back to the beach where he started his journey it seemed to be further away than any distant memory. "Once past the reef the water level drops off, like crazy deep man, maybe a hundred feet and just keeps going down into the bottom of the world," the surfer dude had also relayed to him without prompting, almost as if the guy could tell what he was planning for the next night's activities. The bottom of the world was his destination.

Bringing his attention back to the reef he struggled crab-like against the breakers. Finally, he came to the other edge of the reef, feeling the lip with his toes, fighting with all his might to keep hold against the lash of the ocean. He was bathed in darkness and shivering, the surging wind chilling the rivulets of salt water that ran along his skin. The shrills sent jolts tightening his muscles in anticipation. There were late summer nights when he was a young teenager clad in just cut off denim shorts, horsing around in his friend's pool, when he would be standing on the deck dripping wet and freezing, then jumping back under. The warmness of the water exquisitely enveloping him. That experience was as close as he had come to an orgasmic sensation, at the time. That's what he was hoping for now, that the black warm sea would just carry him away like a comfortable dream.

Just a few more deep breaths. He wasn't hesitating. No, he was ready. He was just preparing himself, sizing up the situation. Allen was just tingling with the desire to penetrate into his patient mistress.

Other odd thoughts about his past suddenly came to him in fleeting unconnected bursts like green static. Stuff he couldn't sort out, isolated things that didn't make much sense floating in his peripheral mind-sight. Now was not the time to be cataloging bits and pieces of his pathetic life. It was time to go. Allen tried to scatter the thoughts.

He waited for the next crash of a wave to surge past his body and he pushed out with all his legs had, like when he would be diving off of the platform above a pool, dissecting the lane of water separated by lengths of bobbed blue and white ropes. For that one instant in midair he was transformed to the moment when he had lunged at the sound of the starter pistol with three hundred of his classmates, friends and parents cheering him on, urging him to swim his best, win the race, see the lighted amber numbers on the time clock and know that there was nobody faster, thrown his hands up in triumph as Mr. Hanraity jumped into the pool with his suit and tie on to hug him, and saw the majority of the Montpelier High School student body going out of their minds with excitement. It was the greatest feeling ever. But the heady image only lasted for that brief flash.

When he hit the water, cutting into the heart of a wave, the force of the swirling current torqued his torso so severely that it tore the external oblique muscles in his side sending a machete stab of agony through his body. Allen swam despite the pain. The water rose and fell in tremendous swells as he channeled all his energy into the choreo-graphed motion of performance swimming. But the ocean was different from the placid stillness of a pool. The pressure of the surging sea exhausted him quickly and he felt his momentum depleting. Salt water slapped his face from both directions and he could not manage the regulated breathing he used when swimming laps. Every way he turned to take a breath the sea filled his mouth.

Abandoning all prospects of a controlled swim Allen went full bore into the depths of the black lady, arms yanking him forward, legs pumping, thrusting, gasping, his muscles burning. He neared the point of no return. His final release into her.

And Allen remembered the first time he had experienced those sensations with a girl, the summer before his senior year. His dad had a business trip in Columbus and he acknowledged that Allen was old enough to be on his own for a couple of days, eighteen in three months, so he could take his mom, make it a long weekend away from the small-town life. Not that Columbus was a major cultural metropolis but there were some nicer restaurants than the local Applebee's and they could see a show at the Palace Theater, maybe visit the museum, some shopping, whatever. They left him with a laundry list of things he couldn't do, like no parties, no alcohol, no sleepovers; gave him a stern talking to about responsibilities, and left him sixty bucks to buy pizzas and kissed him goodbye. Allen spent Friday night with Steve and a few of his other buddies playing loud music in the basement, drinking beer and acting somewhat rebellious without actually setting the couch on fire, but he had bigger plans for the next night. Lisa, his girlfriend since the school Valentine's dance, told her parents that she was staying overnight at her friend Jenny's, but with Jenny's help she snuck out and went over to Allen's house. He let her in his kitchen door, off the darkened back porch and kissed her, awash with relief and renewed anticipation. They eagerly went upstairs. It was the first time for both of them and they undressed each other with shaky fingers and crawled together under the sheets of his bed. The sex was awkward but satisfying in its unexplored originality and afterwards, lying naked in each other's arms and talking like real lovers, was the happiest he had been in his life. There was a powerful thrill secreted away when he told his parents, upon their return, that his weekend had been uneventful.

All those emotions suddenly came back to him in a wash of forgotten joy as the memories flooded up from his subconscious.

Just a few minutes of excruciating exercise had ravaged his body. His legs cramped, the sockets of his shoulders were rusting joints of an unoiled machine, his head pounded and God did his side hurt.

Had he gone far enough? He'd lost all track of time and distance. The ocean, she did things like that to you. She absorbed you in the vastness of her influence so that you forgot where you were. Was he deep enough so that he would drift out to sea and be forgotten? Couldn't tell. Maybe a few more strokes. Ten more. Five. One.

Allen brought his exhausted arms to his side, scissoring his legs to stay afloat, bobbing with the swells. This was it. In a few seconds he would plunge down into the blackness. Should there be a prayer? A concluding thought? Some gesture to put a climax on his final adventure? As he was contemplating this, the undertow of a passing wave sucked him under and he gulped in the salty fragrance of the sea that he had tasted once in his past. More of those unconnected recollections fused together in his mind.

To a time when he was a young boy of eight and he was at the beach for the very first time, his introduction to the seductress. As in all little kids when regarding older women, he never noticed her sensuality or power. He was in Florida on vacation visiting his father's brother, Uncle Nick, who lived in Daytona. With his parents lounging on a beach blanket nearby his uncle took him to the edge of the sand and tried to explain to him how to body surf in the strong tide of the waves as they rolled into the beach.

"Make your body rigid, keep your arms extended and up and slip right into the middle of a wave and you'll ride her in just like a surfboard. Watch me."

His uncle walked out into waist high water and timed his lunge into a wave and with his pot belly bulging out over his shorts, damned if he didn't pull it off with an extraordinary amount of grace. Well, if this fat old guy could do it then so could he. Allen waded through to a point as far in as his uncle had gone, sized up the breaking rolls and leaped forward. But he misjudged the wave speed and jumped too soon. The water threw his legs over his head and he triple-flipped, sucking in foam and flopping onto the shore looking like a pathetic sand-snowman, globs of beige ooze caked in his ears, hair and bathing suit. Allen abruptly threw up the contents of his stomach, mostly salt water but some sliced bananas and milky cereal as well. Laughing so hard he had to hold his gut to prevent pulling a muscle his uncle managed to quip, "Kid, you sure do things the hard way." It wasn't pleasant but it was definitely memorable. His mom took him up the beach to the house and cleaned the sludge and puke from his face with the garden hose. Allen went running right back out there to try again and had mastered the art of body surfing ten minutes later. His uncle bought him a 'Jim Dandy' sundae at Friendly's that

Bursting from the ocean he tried to pull in a fast breath but another wave was assaulting him, smashing him in the ear, spiraling him sideways and he was gone again.

It was a wicked punch to the side of his head, sting and throb combined, but he managed to recover and stagger back into the fracas. The war was only a couple of seconds old but the fighting had been intense. They all had met at the agreed upon time and place; 3:15 after classes, the back of the school around where the cafeteria's extension boxed in a rear courtyard that held the stained and battered garbage bins and the chained bicycles of the janitorial staff. There was just the one door that was used by the kitchen crew to dump the bags of refuse from half eaten lunch trays. They knew they wouldn't be disturbed. Thomas, Eddie and Richie were the school screw ups. Outcast from every clique, they formed their own; the mean bastards who liked to single out anyone who was non-athletic or a social loner and make their life miserable. It was senior year and by now nearly everyone had a group of friends that you hung with, but a new kid, Miles, had just moved into the area and he was short and a little nerdy and didn't fit in, not even with the other nerds. It was only a month into the school year and Miles had been robbed of his lunch money several times, bounced off the padded walls of the gym and had his books airmailed down the stairs among many other milder persecutions. One morning Allen saw the three goons bunched in around Miles pinning him into his open locker. A teacher was at the far end of the hall, Mrs. Shanter, but she was loaded down with paraphernalia and not paying attention. On impulse Allen screamed out "Why don't you three shitheads leave the kid alone!" The corridor went dead silent. Everyone knew he had said it except for the teacher whose gaze came up and caught the three in the act of the assault. She quickly stomped down to the locker and confronted them.

"Is there a problem here?"

"No, Mrs. Shanter," Thomas replied for all of them.

But Miles had a hard-fought-against tear in the corner of his eye and she instantly caught the implication, connecting it with the reputation of the trio.

"Detention, all three of you, for the rest of the week. I'll give the vice principal your names."

She handed some of her things to Miles and asked him to help her carry them to her classroom which effectively removed him from harm's way and the three knew she would be peppering him with all kinds of questions about what had been happening. They were busted big time.

When Mrs. Shanter and Miles had vacated the hall the three looked at him with venomous eyes.

The following week the word came to him that he had an appointment with them after school. Allen went, he wasn't one to back down from a fight, but he wasn't stupid either, he didn't go alone. He took Steve, his best friend, and another friend, Dave.

The thugs seemed kind of surprised that he hadn't come by himself and Thomas was mouthing off and Allen thought the best this bully could muster was a verbal tongue lashing, Eddie and Richie standing in the background also cursing him out. When they were finally face to face, Allen was a couple inches taller but twenty pounds lighter than Thomas, he said, "What's the matter, am I a little too big for you to pick on?" Thomas stood there for several seconds pursing his pale lips, contemplating and just when he thought the punk was about to back down, he swung, and Allen hadn't expected it.

Steve charged into the space that Allen had flailed back from and caught Thomas in the gut with his shoulder and they went sprawling. Dave put a head lock on Eddie, and he rallied jumping onto Richie. It was mostly close quarter fighting, grabbing and grappling. He'd caught a shot in the ribs but managed a potent jab into Richie's solar plex and he went down hard. Steve was still wrestling with Thomas and Allen yanked his friend free. Eddie had taken one punch to the face and fled. Thomas stood up, his shirt collar ripped with a scarlet welt on his neck. He looked and saw Richie on his side moaning and Eddie's tail lights headed for home and knew he was beaten. Slowly Allen closed the space between them. It appeared like Thomas was going to mutter some kind of surrender or apology but before he could Allen slapped him, open palm in the face. The smack stunned him, his face crumpling as if he was going to wail like an infant. He backed away, helped Richie to his feet and they were gone. The three heroes went to Steve's garage, soaked their knuckles in a cooler full of ice and Mountain Dews, and laughed as they recounted the bout, blow by blow, elevating the exaggeration factor with each telling. That afternoon he felt more like one of the boys than he had ever felt before. Friends. He had real 'stick their neck on the line for you' friends. It was an awesome feeling.

He was fighting again, to reach the surface, fighting for breath. Pushing his head up he managed a gasp but waves were assaulting him from every direction and he had to spit out a mouthful of inky salt before he could suck in air. Somehow, he didn't think it would be like this. This intense. He was hoping for an end more along that of his mother's when she faded off into oblivion without really knowing she was going. How could dying be such a struggle? Although he couldn't see it, Allen sensed the next melee. A massive wave. A big slow one, rolling in over him. The culminating sound was consuming. This was it - the lady had him by the balls.

Breaking up with Lisa was hard on him. They had spent most of the summer vacation together. They spent many steamy nights parked in his car in any secluded spot they could find to have half-dressed sex. There was something different though once school started and he sensed the change but ignored it. It was the week before Thanksgiving when she approached him at lunch and they sat alone in the bleachers of the gymnasium. Her face was clenched as she firmly held his hand. He listened and dreaded what was coming.

"You already know what you're going to do with your life. You've got decent grades and you're going to get a scholarship for swimming for sure. Some big school will give you an offer and you'll be off to sunny Florida or California and you're going to do great. But me...I got no skills. My grades are just passing and a college career is not in my future. What I do have is a chance to go to Europe over Christmas recess with Jenny and her family. My parents agreed to pay for the trip as my present. I've always wanted to go to Italy and see the sights. And I haven't told anyone this so please keep it to yourself but I probably won't be coming back. I'm just going to take off and live there for a couple of years and get some worldly experience. But I can't do any of that if I have somebody back here who's waiting for me to return. I think it's best if we just stay friends. You'll always be special to me because...you were my first, and maybe someday...but who knows. Until then...I really have to be on my own."

She kissed him goodbye and just like that it was done. His buds helped him out, getting him beer and getting him drunk and telling him that she wasn't worth it and he was better off without her and eventually his life went on. With nothing much to do that Christmas and desperate not to think about Lisa in Italy he wound up going to his father's company holiday party and saw the girl of his dreams. She had on a red knit sweater dress that clung to her curves as if painted on, hem high on her thigh with one bare shoulder exposed. Allen stared at her and he caught her glancing back, smiling and he thought he would stain his pants on the spot. He didn't think it would go much beyond that but then his father called him over and introduced her to him. Her name was Colleen and she was the secretary of his dad's manager. They made some small talk in which he mumbled like an idiot and then she announced, when the DJ started a song, that it was her favorite and she dragged him onto the dance floor. They stayed up there for two fast songs and then she snuggled up to him when a ballad came on.

"How do you think your father would react if I asked him if I could take you home with me?"

Allen jerked his head back to look into her eyes, see if she was kidding. She most definitely was not.

"How old are you?" he asked.

"Why? Does it matter?"

"I don't know. I guess it doesn't."

"Would my age influence your decision?"

"No," he replied without hesitation.

"Twenty-six."

"Wow."

"So how do we work this?" she queried, eyebrows raised.

But he was already planning.

"Listen dad, I promised Steve I would go bowling with him tonight. They're having a Christmas thing at Bryan Lanes and he's going to pick me up outside in five minutes. OK?" His dad was a little disappointed but he agreed as long as there was no drinking. "And we might be getting back late so I'm just going to sleep at Steve's." Again, his dad was less than enthusiastic but allowed it. He thanked him, shook his hand, kissed his mom and was out the door. He ran to the 7-11 two blocks down, his scheduled meeting place with Colleen, called Steve and collaborated the cover story. Allen bought a pack of rubbers, Dentyne gum, a stick of deodorant which he used and threw away and a rose in a clear plastic sleeve. Fifteen minutes later he was getting antsy thinking maybe she had played a practical joke on him when she pulled up in a silver sport Benz.

"Sorry. It took me forever to say my goodbyes," she said as she stepped out of the car, her unbuttoned coat swaying. He handed her the rose and she kissed him and handed him the keys. "What's this for?"

"I'm slightly drunk. You drive."

Could this night get any better? The car was new and sleek and beautiful and drove like a purring kitten. Colleen closed her eyes and he had to focus on the GPS and his driving even though his sight kept wandering to her bare legs. If he had to, he would have been content to drive all night with this gorgeous girl and his Christmas would have been the best ever. They pulled up to her apartment building twenty minutes later. The short napped had renewed her verve as she took his hand and tethered him to the elevator where she pinned him to the wall with her kiss as the doors closed and everything went up. Inside her apartment she took his jacket, directed him over to the couch and pushed him into a sitting position. Then she proceeded to strip off her coat and clothes. In her red bra and panties, she was stunning but when she popped them off and dropped them on the floor next to the dress, Allen was afraid to look away or blink that she would disappear. But she was there and she was so beautiful he thought he might pass out. Walking towards him in only her high heels Allen felt his body humming uncontrollably. Colleen yanked him up, spun him and sat down on the couch, her legs devilishly crossed bouncing the shiny black pump up and down and instructed him, "Now it's your turn." Allen peeled off his clothes piece by piece and when naked she made him turn his lean, hard swimmer's physique slowly around. "This is what I had imagined when I first saw you tonight." She uncrossed her legs and hooked her finger at him.

An exhausted ecstasy that was unmatched left his body limp. She did things to him that no one had ever done before. Two hours later they were still in the living room lying on the soft maroon rug. He had an arm folded under his head, staring down at Colleen who was lying between his legs, her head resting on his lower stomach, eyes closed but not sleeping. His gaze tracked from her long blond hair, down her back, over her smooth globe of an ass and continued the length of shapely legs and delicate feet. Lisa had been cute that one time he had actually seen her completely nude but Colleen had a body that sculptures needed to sculpt, painters wanted to paint, and he had had. At this point in his life, he didn't have a clue what the difference between love and lust was but tonight they were one in the same.

"Do you know how weird it was for me to say goodnight to your father when I left that party, knowing I was about to seduce his son," she commented without moving or opening her eyes.

For a few moments he said nothing then, "I want to sleep with you."

She turned her head, raising mischievous eyebrows.

"No, I mean I want to go into your bed and wrap you in my arms and hold you all night. Your skin up against mine, my lips on you. I want to burn you into my memory. I don't ever want to forget your body, this night or the love we've shared."

Colleen blinked repeatedly, tears leaking from the corner of her eyes, she swallowed hard and he felt the motion of her neck in his groin. She opened her mouth twice but nothing came out. On the third try she said, "No one has ever said anything that wonderful to me before."

She crawled up his body and kissed him with a passion he had not known was possible. Hand in hand they walked to her bedroom, made love again and did exactly what he had said. Laying on him she slowly pulled the white sheet up over their naked entwined forms and covered them.

But the black sheet of water that covered him now would not rise. Eternity embraced him, crushing in all around him and he felt his body going down as if it had been strapped to the floor of a descending elevator. He couldn't tell how far down he had gone but it felt like the whole hundred feet he had been warned about. At any second, he expected to be planted into the silt on the bottom. He was lost in liquid space.

This was exactly what he had planned. And now, wanted no part of.

All those wonderful memories. How could he have forgotten them? And it wasn't just those. It was his mom's golden crusted apple pie which she served with sharp cheddar cheese on top rather than ice cream. And his dad showing up the one time he'd tried to put together a band and they had an impromptu concert out of Steve's garage that six people attended and his dad stood there, bobbed his head to the music even though Allen knew he hated it. The Christmas he'd gotten his Hot Wheels City that he had begged Santa for, and was so excited he played with it for nearly every waking minute for the following two weeks. Kissing Rosalia Parone on the schoolyard jungle gym on the last day of fifth grade as it was starting to rain.

There were so many exploding in his head so quickly he could only gleam minor details from more elaborate images. The lush green grass of his backyard, Steve's garage couch with its hidden sleeve for Playboys, catching a dirt covered baseball, happy tears on his mom's cheeks, a new pencil on his first day of school, a vacation dinner in Montreal, a tree fort, bathtub bubbles, a red bike, his toes, a sparkler, toast. About a million more were hovering just outside these others waiting for a chance to squeeze in and get their turn.

Week after week, months into years of burdensome thoughts about that one atrocious period of his life had weighed down every breath he took with blackened despair. The traumatic impact had shoved the entirety of his past wonderful life into a vault. Suddenly the hinges on the vault had corroded away and the door fell off with a resounding thump of gray steel and like Pandora's Box, everything flew out with crazed abandonment to parade shamelessly around his mind. Not only those memories but he also recalled so many missed opportunities when he could have enjoyed an experience or a conversation with another person, even the simple contact of one lonely human reaching out to another and for the past dozen years he'd shunned every single occasion. Wasted. His brain pinpointed a thousand, maybe a hundred thousand, chances that could have led him back, even if it was only a baby step, onto the path of redemption. All those times were tainted with the stain of his parents' death. He had been so blind.

But his blindness, floating in the black water below the black sky had been penetrated by a metaphorical ray of light, burning white and beautiful and perhaps it was the light of hope but he feared it was the face of God. Maybe they were one in the same. Maybe...

In an eruption of red-hot desire Allen started ripping through arm after arm of water, tearing for the surface but--he didn't know if he was moving up or down. So many times, he'd been turned and flipped that he had no sense of direction. He wanted to stop and analyze the situation but there was no time. His lungs had reached their limit and were about to breathe in the sea. 'Just go in the direction you're pointed,' his mind ordered him. Allen obeyed.

He rose from the depths like a flirtatious dolphin, his whole body cresting the waves and he breathed in air, sweet air that never filled his lungs just so perfectly. There he hung suspended for a moment, his chest filling to its capacity, thanking God for His wonderful gift of oxygen. But gravity sent him crashing down into the surf, a whale breaching the water from either side of him. He was back in the vicious ocean. And all at once he realized he'd tapped out his strength. Cold blue fear made him sick. His muscles had been pushed to their limit and he'd drawn every ounce of adrenalin from his system. The tanks were empty. Allen managed a few feeble flaps of his arms keeping him afloat for a couple of seconds of rapid breathing and he went down again.

The water became quicksand dragging his leaden limbs into the void. He punished his body into moving and managed a minor reprieve but it would not be for long. The waves pounded onto his head like hammer blows, each assault sucking more of the life out of him. Time and again he struggled mightily to the surface for a quick breath only to be submerged forcefully once more. The sea wove around him at will as if the wicked bitch were caressing him in her clutches. She liked watching him suffer. Playing with him as a cat toys with a captured mouse until it gets bored and just swallows it. The next surge up he stroked so slowly he felt he wouldn't have reached the other side if he'd been in a bathtub. He held his head aloft for a short couple of seconds scanning the horizon. The sky had dropped its full blackness on top of the sea and wiped out every glimmer of light in all directions. There was no way to tell where the land was.

He screamed at the top of his lungs but a weak moan was all he could muster. His original plan was working to perfection. Exhaustion had overtaken him and he was in a position that he couldn't recover from. There might be no other choice but to go through with this after all. Tears hadn't a chance under these conditions to run their obligatory course down his cheeks, they were obliterated by the constant spray of the sea but a third liquid now circulated on his face; rain. The clouds that had been threatening all evening had decided to choose now to relieve themselves on him and help fill the ocean a little bit more. Big heavy drops that might have also been black for all he knew, pelted his brow. Water sucking his life from below, water beating from above. Yet, was the stinging rain another gift from God? Needling into his face, waking him up, keeping him alive, forcing him to think.

Twisted about, Allen felt like a blindfolded child with a donkey pin-tail in his fingers and there was no wall to be found. Which of a hundred directions should he take? He had to make a decision and he had to try. Barely he clung to the surface having no clue what source of strength fueled him. The storm intensified, harder rain, sharper waves driving white caps of sea into his nostrils. Swirling listlessly away from the sanctuary of air once more, he felt the motion of the waves pulling him down without resistance. Queen Neptune had decided for him. She was taking him to her lair on the ocean floor.

Allen wondered what the final sensation would feel like as he tumbled away. Would it be cinematic in its scope, consuming him with angel choirs and endless puffy clouds, transforming him into utter whiteness? Or perhaps it would be more of disassembling of his atoms and neurons, being flung out in all possible directions to mingle among the stars. When it came upon him it wasn't what he expected at all. Pain. His back cracked as if he had been struck by the mace of a giant. A million little knives stabbed into his skin. Lungs imploding, rib cage crushing, head exploding with the impact. Gruesome end.

Then in a flash of realization he knew what the sea had flung him into. The side of the reef. He had found his wall. Desperately grasping the sharp corals, he spun his body around so he could try and climb up but the backlash of the tide had pulled him away and he was clawing at empty water. He tried vainly to swim forward but he felt as if he were being dragged backwards by his ankles. Desperation devoured his last bit of hope, chewing on it like a piece of dry steak. One last memory that had been hanging around now slid into his consciousness.

The hospital smelled of disinfectant but it couldn't mask the odor of death that permeated every corner of the room where his father lay grimacing in his sleep. For the past couple of days, the drugs seemed to have little effect and his dad was in constant pain. His mom was also sleeping, on the uncomfortable orange chair in the corner. She looked like a black and white photograph of herself, all shades of uncomplimentary grays. The person who had taken this photo of her saw that it was not a good likeness and had crumpled it up. Allen turned back to stare out the window. The rest of the world was out there enjoying their summer but he was here waiting for a miracle that he knew would never come. A feeling made him turn around and he saw his dad staring at him with vacant eyes and for a second, he thought-

-but then he blinked. He crouched down over the bed because he sensed his dad was going to tell him something.

"What is it dad?"

Speaking in a hoarse whisper his dad had to take a rattling gasp after nearly every word. "I--remember--when you--were born. --I--kissed you."

For the past three weeks Allen had been holding back his tears but he could no longer stem the tide. The raw emotions poured from his eyes dripping down onto the sheets. The single line of speech had depleted his father, sweat prickling up in tiny pools on his forehead, but he had one more thing to relay to him.

"You'll--be--alone--the next--time--but I'll--kiss you--again."

He had gazed at his father's tired eyes, hoping not to show the bewilderment in his face but his dad looked back and revealed a tiny smile and an almost unnoticeable nod of acknowledgment. Those were the last words he spoke on his last day on earth.

There was nobody to hear Allen's last words.

Again, his body went limp with defeat and he let the tide take him to his ultimate resting place. There was just no point in struggling anymore. He was finished. But the surge of the next wave sent him crashing face first into the reef. The blow broke his nose and forced his mouth open and his deprived lungs drank in the cold lava solution, filling his chest with a pain beyond comparison. His hands grappled as those of a maniac but his progression was equal to the speed of slow motion in dreams. The brackish poison of the big blue burned his insides and he felt that his heart must burst.

He came upward off the reef with a sound of exploding air like cannon fire. The wave had ejected him from its depths and spit him out onto the coral bed. Landing on his side, Allen flipped once and his skin was grated into pink pulpy cheese against the piked coral. He was free of the water, trying to regain his sense of awareness but his lungs still held the sea.

And then with all the force of a whale's spout the water came spewing forth. Hugging the living structure like a giant toilet bowl he expelled everything that was inside him until his chest cavity was empty and air came in. It wasn't sweet like before. It burned like acid, pushing the remnants of salt into the membranes of his lung's blood vessels but he would take the agony of that breath over the hell of the sea every second for as long as he could stay alive. Which might not be for long. He heard the next attack coming. The increasing roar of monstrous waves. He tried to brace his knees into any grooves he could find. As he looked for purchase with his hands, he could make out in the darkness that some of his fingers were dislocated into grotesque positions. There was no way he was holding on. The thrust gored him like the horns of a bull and lifted him skyward and again he struck the reef with his back in a spray of red mist. He rolled one more time into a broken crouch, gasping in scorching oxygen. He felt the intense shaking of shock as his body started to overload. Another slap of the lady's fury would destroy him and it was approaching. A crescendo of flexing ocean sucking in all the air and water around it and molding into a gargantuan fist to deliver the final blow. And it exploded like a bomb.

But not on him. The reef absorbed all of its force and he was only peppered with the dying splash of the diminishing wave. He had been thrown so far inside the reef that he was protected by the ancient obstacle as it buffered the swells. Wave after wave threatened menacingly with its tumultuous approach but disintegrated before it could reach him. With whatever support he could muster he held on. His only chance of survival now was to stay in this position until morning and hope someone would notice the pathetic figure clinging to life and he could be rescued. But how long was it until sunrise? It was still night, his only sense of time, and he would have to cower there for hours in his current condition. That was not possible. Blood ran freely from his shattered nose and countless puncture wounds in his skin. He was shivering uncontrollably and hypothermia would be setting in soon. His misshapen hands and toes were cramping from the intense grip on the gnarly coral. He was beaten inside and out. The chance of him lasting the hours until morning was fading, along with his strength and consciousness. How much more did he have left to give? And yet the distant sensation of sunlight was an inspiring notion. Maybe it was the same life-giving light that had etched a beam into his heart. God's little ray of hope again.

Suddenly it went intensely white and he feared his image before of death had come to fruition. He blinked and saw he had not moved upward into the heavens but remained on the reef and then a sound greater than the rushing waves rocked his world. Thunder. The storm had arrived. He realized for the first time since he was cast from the sea that it was not just a diffusion of ocean drenching him but driving rain as well.

Water, water everywhere. How could he have been so miserably misdirected? About everything. Not long ago all he wanted in life, or what he perceived was left of it, was to be one with this lady. Now he wanted to be free of her. But she surrounded him, the waves beckoning him to come back. Her sister, the rain, urging him down with her relentless deluge, thunder and lightning to show proof of their impatience. To highlight his thought a silver streak blanched the sky and for the first time he saw colors other than black. The dark reds and browns that comprised the coral formations and his pale gray skin streaked with ribbons of crimson. He also saw something else he wouldn't have if the sky hadn't been momentarily illuminated. Next to the tip of his malformed pinky, bent sideways at the knuckle, was the placid water of the lagoon. He was perched on the very edge of the reef that had torn his shoulder not long before when he had climbed up to reach the ocean proper. There was just a quarter mile of calm water between himself and the rest of the earth.

Allen actually thought, for a beat, that he could make it if he tried, but just the idea of using any strength almost made him vomit and he dismissed that as a solution. His tortured mind could no longer operate. Too many images, memories, questions and emotions had flooded his brain pan. With no motor function, no synapse control and no emotional output Allen's body went limp and toppled to the left over the side of the reef.

The ocean here had retained the heat of the day, filling him with one singular sensation, warmth. The waves were gentle things. A vague recollection of the shore also came to mind and finally an impulse. Swim. With all his heart he tried but the first stroke of his beleaguered muscles sent a tremor of pain through him that was so intense he collapsed beneath the surface. The black was now almost comforting. The experience was completed and it was time to let go.

He was so tired, of firstly trying to die and then trying to live, that he decided to curl up and float away. Allen tucked his arms and legs in and let the lady do with him as she pleased. Heaven or hell, or somewhere in between, as long as he didn't have to labor to get there. The darkness engulfed him, all his senses mixed into one quagmire that blended in with everything around him and it was just totally inviolable black. He was nothing. A huddled nothing.

He unexpectedly bobbed to the surface and took a breath, a slow unhurried breath. Without opening his eyes or trying to maneuver he wafted there until his lungs were sated and then he sank below the water line again. An unfathomable amount of time passed and he came up again and breathed again and submersed again. Oscillating between air and sea fell into a smooth rhythm. There was no thought or muscle gesture. No effort or emotion. It went instinctively on, a gray-pink naked fetus in a warm wet womb with nothing to do but breath and wait and let nature take its course.

The sensation on his cheek was wonderful. A warm wet kiss that he wished would never stop. Not a kiss, more of a lick. Other less pleasing sensations quickly filtered in however, overriding the goodness. Grit and a sour saltiness in his swollen mouth and nose, a throbbing, resonating up the back of his neck, pulsing out of his ears and pounding into his skull, a burn in his chest that seared his lungs with each breath, and tenuous pain everywhere. Allen forced his crusted eyes open and saw the sand stained terracotta red with his dried blood. His limbs were stone frozen in contracted positions. He swiveled his eyes to the side and caught the image of an elongated nose and wonderful pink tongue lapping the side of his face. A tattered dog continued the adoration to his cheek. Then Allen moved and an unnatural scream exploded from his lips. That only good feeling stopped completely, the dog backing away from the noise.

Allen was on his side and the exertion required in attempting to roll onto his back was shattering, sending wrenching spasms of pain into every ripped muscle. But like an infant trying for the first time, he contorted his torso to complete the quarter rotation. It took several long agonizing seconds before he could lower his back onto the beach and the simple motion, coupled with the sting of the gravely surface on his shredded skin, nearly caused him to pass out. The painful exercise did however affirm his existence. And as he stared up into the heavens, there was the light. It was a gray-orange glow coming up from somewhere on the other side of the island. Though the dawn was almost unseeable, it was not blackness and he never appreciated the light of day more than at that moment. God's way of telling him 'Good morning to the rest of your life.' He endured a little more pain and rotated his head further and saw an old, cream-colored dog sitting awkwardly on the tilt of the land gazing at him with familiar eyes. Tired eyes. The dog that had kissed him flexed his jowls in the semblance of a tiny smile and nodded his head, almost unnoticeably, then turned and vanished into the shrubs at the opening of the beach.

From the space the dog had vacated Allen could see the tranquil blue waters of the lagoon in the distance. There was no more storm and the gentle sea rolled in and faded away without care. How he had emerged from her was a mystery.

The lady lay there unchanged by the event.

But he had been changed. He'd been excruciatingly reformed. Torn apart and reconstructed. Emotionally and physically. The waters of life had christened his bloody rebirth. He'd been given the rare gift of a second chance. The possibilities began to fill his head with rapture. There was so much he had to do if he could just get his ravaged body up off the beach. It would not be an easy task but he was willing to try.

But first, to the sea, he acknowledged a note of thanks for her part in his revival. He would forever have a reverence for her that he would always cherish. But from afar.

REDEMPTIVE WATERS

DAVID LANGE

January 6, 1810. Thirty-eight degrees, twenty minutes, North latitude; sixty-five degrees, thirty-seven minutes, West longitude [north of Bermuda]. Making six knots on a North by Northeast heading. *HMS Phoebe*, having sustained significant damage during the Battle of Trafalgar, some five years before, was, much like her captain, struggling to prove her worth and avoid the inevitable demise that all but the most historic vessels ultimately succumb to. Captain Charles Grainger had shared the seas, off Cape Trafalgar, with the legendary Admiral Horatio Nelson as he defeated the combined French and Spanish fleet, thereby putting an end to Napoleon Bonaparte's ambitions for a cross-channel invasion and subjugation of England. Nelson lost his life in the engagement but saved his nation and altered the course of European history forever. Grainger, in command of the sleek thirty-six-gun frigate, *HMS Phoebe*, kept his life but lost an arm and a leg as he expertly maneuvered his warship amidst the raining cannonball fire of supremely more powerful first and second-rate vessels, boasting upward of ninety to a hundred guns, including the hull-smashing 36-pounder cannons on their lower decks. *Phoebe* had but one gun deck, versus the three gun-laden decks of the capital ships, but Grainger knew that speed and gun accuracy could help offset what the frigate, as a fifth-rate vessel, lacked in firepower. Trafalgar was the pinnacle of Captain Grainger's distinguished naval career. And now he was waiting to die.

It wasn't his unchecked alcoholism that proved to be Captain Grainger's downfall but instead his fervent critiques of the Crown's colonial aspirations and often hard-handed methods for growing the Empire. Were it not for his expert seamanship and tenuous familial connection to several notable nobles who were, themselves, on the decline, it's likely that Grainger might have lived out his days in some ramshackle alehouse in Ipswich. The Admiralty, as it seems, was not without pity. They granted Grainger command, once more, of HMS Phoebe, now sadly relegated to the role of training vessel. She was but a shell of her former self. Half the guns had been removed and transferred to newer vessels and the remaining cannon were desperately in need of refurbishment. The hull, encrusted with barnacles and plagued by failing timbers, was in even greater need of an overhaul. Still, for all that, the vessel served admirably as a training platform for the young crew. Some of the cadets had aspirations to pass for officers and, one day, become the next Lord Horatio Nelson while others were pleased just to remain free of the prisons and workhouses.

Now several months at sea, neither the ship's officers nor the crew had seen much of the elusive Captain Grainger except for those times when he appeared upon the quarterdeck to run his charges through grueling exercises in gunnery, sail adjustments, and the like. Grainger, for reasons he kept to himself, preferred to wander the deck at night. During the day, his first mate, Jonathan Randolph, and second mate, Andrew Carnehall, ran the young cadets through navigation exercises and basic seamanship drills in addition to exposing them to a varied curriculum which included everything from basic mathematics to literature and music. Captain Grainger believed that a well-rounded education set the young sailors on a truer course toward proficiency at sea and success in life. Ever loyal, it must be said that even Lieutenants Randolph and Carnehall considered their captain to be a bit of an enigma. He emanated a kind of burning intensity that encouraged others to keep their distance. Yet, on those occasions when he stood upon the quarterdeck in command of his vessel, there seemed something almost mythological about his presence. And then, much to his disgust, his vulnerability would be on full display as he fumbled with his telescope, struggling to extend it with his one hand while gripping the device in his armpit. His wooden peg leg, likewise, frustrated him in rough seas. Staggering about from one position to the next, on the pitching and rolling deck, Captain Grainger would pound his fist in rage against the masts, cursing his disability. To his crew, his physical challenges made him more rather than less human. The roar of cannon fire from past engagements had severely damaged his hearing and a cancer in his lungs was slowly eating away at what little time he had left to live. While a few of the youngest boys might mock their mysterious leader, a stern eye from the able-bodied seamen onboard would set them straight. Upon this wooden island, there was but one master and his orders were second only to God's.

Making their way north toward Halifax, *HMS Phoebe* found herself in rough seas which was not uncommon given the time of year. Captain Grainger ordered the crew to reduce sail and replace the existing sails with the more robust storm sails. Lieutenant Randolph looked on, nervously, as the young student crew carefully worked their way up the ice-covered ratlines and struggled to maintain a grip as they slid along the yardarms of the three-masted frigate. It was not a pretty operation and Captain Grainger returned to his cabin to smoke his pipe, filled with frustration yet understanding that his cadet crew was unlikely to match the well-trained synchronization of his veteran crew at Trafalgar. "What would Nelson say, had he witnessed the sloppy exchange of sails?" he thought. "An embarrassment to king and crown. Tomorrow we shall work to right this situation." He muttered to himself, in-between his coughing, as he pondered his fate as captain of a training ship.

Throughout the night, *HMS Phoebe* was tossed about upon the unforgiving sea, taking on more than her share of water as the aged timbers of the hull strained to maintain their integrity. The sailors from the previous watch wanted nothing more than to curl up in their hammocks though their clothes were yet soaked in the bone-chilling waters of the Atlantic. However, with water rising below decks, all able-bodied hands manned the bilge pumps to extract the unwanted seawater and return it to its rightful home. The sun had barely broken the horizon before the sailing master was hard at work trying to ascertain the *Phoebe's* position as the storm had clearly blown her well east of her planned track toward Nova Scotia. From high atop the crow's nest, a cry rang out—"Ship ahoy!"

"Where away?" shouted the first mate from below.

"Half a league off the starboard bow, Sir," came the reply. Lieutenant Randolph had hardly trained his glass upon the speck on the horizon before the captain was on deck, straining his ageing eyes to make out the nature of the stationary vessel in the distance. Fumbling with his brass telescope, Captain Grainger studied the scene. The second mate, Andrew Carnehall, joined the captain and first mate on the quarterdeck whereupon Lieutenant Randolph passed his telescope so that he might try his eye at identifying the ship.

"What do you make of her, Andrew?" asked the first mate.

"She's only got a single mast but she's clearly flying the colors of England." Lieutenant Randolph motioned to Carnehall to return his telescope so that he might continue his assessment and Captain Grainger, who had already completely and accurately assessed the situation, listened to his officers with interest.

"She appears to be a brig, Captain," said Lieutenant Randolph to his superior. "Clearly, she must have lost a mast in the tempest. She looks in bad shape and it's a right fortunate twist of fate that the same storm should carry us into a position where we might render some assistance."

"Right you are, Mister Randolph. By the looks of her, perhaps the *Conquest* or *Resolute*. Where I will stand to differ is on your assessment of the damage."

"How do you mean, Captain?" replied Randolph.

"Examine the mast, Jonathan," began Captain Grainger. No storm could have sheared it off so elegantly. Look, too, upon her larboard side . . . so much as I can see from our vantage point, she appears to have taken some heavy fire. And, on the surviving mast and yardarms, both the mainsail and topsail are severely torn. You've seen storm damage before and these tears appear quite different, do they not?"

"Aye, Captain," replied Lieutenant Randolph as he focused his telescope to further inspect the details Captain Grainger was describing. "Chainshot, Sir?"

"Precisely, Jon! The storm sails were never set. These wounds preceded the storm. Whoever wreaked this terrible damage upon the brig clearly meant to send her below the waves. It's quite the miracle she's still afloat." Captain Grainger coughed fitfully, interrupting his fascinating lesson and alarming his officers who were greatly concerned for their captain's well-being. "Helmsman, set a course for the brig," shouted Captain Grainger after clearing his throat multiple times so that his voice might confidently project toward the sailor minding the ships wheel.

"Aye aye, Captain!" responded the helmsman.

"And, Mister Randolph," the captain whispered to his first mate, "I'll need you to push the crew in drill this afternoon. They've got to be much more proficient in the rigging and I need their gunnery to be quick and impeccably accurate."

"Aye, Captain," responded Randolph.

"And let's run through a couple 'beat to quarters' exercises."

"Aye, Captain, we'll make England proud."

"I'm sure we will," replied Captain Grainger, his stern demeanor concealing the sense of unease he felt about the situation. Years upon the sea had provided him with a unique ability to read the veiled machinations of fate. He buttoned his overcoat against the cold and admired the vaporous plume of his condensing breath as it met the cold winter air.

As the *Phoebe* approached the disabled brig, Captain Grainger's initial assessment was confirmed. She was the 12-gun brig, *HMS Conquest*. The distress signal flags were clearly visible along with several others that the crew did not immediately recognize.

"Signals to take effect after close of the day?" asked Randolph of his Captain. "I don't understand why they'd be flying that flag." The captain considered the question and managed to belay the knowing smile that had requested permission to come aboard.

"That's white over black, Jonathan. When flown upside down, the black bar over white bar means something quite different."

"I'm afraid I'm unfamiliar, Sir."

"Secret instruction, Mister Randolph. It signals 'secret instruction' and that we've stumbled upon what may be a unique opportunity to serve king and country."

"Interesting."

"Interesting, indeed. All the same, I'd prefer you keep this between us until we can better assess the situation," added Captain Grainger.

"Of course, Sir," replied Randolph. The captain nodded his acknowledgment.

Captain Grainger's wooden leg thudded rhythmically upon the wooden planks as he paced about the deck. When slowly closing to within a hundred yards, he signaled for his speaking trumpet and hailed *HMS Conquest*. "Ahoy there! This is Captain Charles Grainger of *His Majesty's Ship Phoebe*. May I have permission from your captain to send a boat over to inquire as to your situation?" Captain Grainger had to wait for his reply but it came soon enough from a nervous voice.

"Ahoy there, Captain Grainger, this is Lieutenant Reginald Whitaker, acting captain of *HMS Conquest*. Our Captain, the honorable Sydney Cross, God rest his soul, was killed in action but two days ago. Your assistance could not be more welcome. We stand ready to receive your party, at your leisure, Sir."

Captain Grainger gathered several of his officers as a boat was prepared on the starboard side. Along with the first mate, surgeon and surgeon's mate, Grainger included the ship's carpenter, sailmaker, and quartermaster. The seamen carefully lowered the boat into the sea where the sailors took the oars to row the party over to the heavily damaged brig.

Captain Grainger and his party were cheerfully welcomed with rousing applause as they came on board. The blood from the recent battle still stained the deck. Immediately, the surgeon and surgeon's mate assisted in tending to the injured while the carpenter and sailmaker assessed the damage to the vessel, considering what options might be available to return her to a seaworthy status.

Captain Grainger and Lieutenant Randolph were welcomed into the captain's quarters by the still visibly shaken Lieutenant Whitaker. While enjoying a cup of tea, the lieutenant explained how they were heading north from South America when they were engaged by two

Spanish frigates—the heavy frigate, *Indomable*, with 46 guns, and the 34-gun frigate *Fama*. While the brig was fast, the frigates appeared upwind in the early morning hours and thus had the "weather gage" advantage of being able to attack with the wind filling their sails. Before the *Conquest* could come about to flee its attackers, as its 12 guns were no match for the more powerful frigates, a broadside of chainshot shredded her sails. The second broadside from *Indomable* dismasted the brig's mizzen mast and put her in great jeopardy. The day appeared lost until a large fog bank provided an opportunity for escape. The injured *Conquest* limped northward until the storm finished the job that two Spanish frigates could not. Short of crew, leaking like a sieve, and with barely enough usable canvas to partially cover two sail positions, she was effectively stranded.

Captain Grainger carefully considered the story and, more so, the notion that two Spanish frigates might still be patrolling the area. With a student crew and only eighteen of the frigate's 36 guns onboard, he knew the odds would not be in his favor in an encounter with the Spanish ships although he was confident that *HMS Phoebe* would fare better than the brig. However, unlike *Conquest*, *HMS Phoebe* lacked the speed advantage over the newer Spanish frigates that might permit her to avoid the mismatched engagement altogether. After assessing the risk, he awaited the more intriguing story that the cryptic signal flags had betrayed. Following an uncomfortable silence, Lieutenant Whitaker got up and walked over to the captain's writing desk whereupon he removed an envelope from the drawer. Captain Grainger could see that the envelope had been sealed with wax, at one point. While the seal was broken, there was no mistaking that a royal crest had secured the contents. Whatever orders resided therein must have been issued from the highest level.

Whitaker handed the envelope to Captain Grainger with a warning that the contents must not be revealed to anyone save, perhaps, his first and second mates. Discretion was of the utmost importance. Captain Grainger carefully unfolded the letter and read the elegantly written note. Whitaker studied the captain's face, anxiously awaiting a reaction, be it a gasp, raised eyebrows, or perhaps even a rousing chorus of Rule Britannia. He was left unsatisfied. Devoid of any expression, Captain Grainger neatly folded the message, returning it to its envelope.

"When may I expect the party?" asked Captain Grainger, as he slid the envelope into his waistcoat.

"With your permission, Captain, I'd like to perform the transfer under the cover of darkness."

"That's acceptable. Now, if you'll excuse me, Lieutenant, I'd like to confer with my inspection team as to their estimates for supplies and labor needed to get you underway. You'll not be wanting to dance with those frigates a second time."

"No, Captain, definitely not. Thank you, Sir."

Meeting upon the deck to discuss the plan, Captain Grainger agreed to the transfer of timber and sail cloth. Despite the carpenter's initial objections, it was also agreed that the carpenter's mate would stay with *HMS Conquest* to aid in expediting repairs to the vessel. For all that, it would likely be several days before she could reliably make headway back to the safety of an English port. Captain Grainger's initial inclination was to provide escort to the damaged brig but his new orders were very specific—he was to make all haste on a return voyage to Portsmouth, England.

Only a few deckhands witnessed the unusual arrival of a small boat in the darkness of the moonless night. Under the lamplight, Lieutenant Whitaker and several sailors expeditiously escorted what appeared to be a well-dressed woman, garbed in a long, hooded cape, aft to the captain's quarters. Shortly thereafter, following a firm handshake and a "good luck and God speed," Whitaker and crew were away and returning to the *Conquest*.

While word spread, the next day, of the strange arrival, the crew of the *Phoebe* knew better than to be caught spreading rumors below deck. That which their captain cared for them to know would, in due course, be revealed and that which he did not share was, quite simply, not worth the knowing. Besides, when the intense sailing and gunnery drills began the next day, there was little time or interest in exchanging scuttlebutt. Empty barrels were cast adrift and guns were loaded, aimed, fired, and re-loaded. Critiqued and re-evaluated, time and time again, the crew honed their skills under the watchful eyes of the observing officers. Speed was critical. Neither Randolph nor Carnehall would settle for any less than three broadsides every five minutes because they knew their captain expected not only that but hair-splitting accuracy as well. It wasn't long before the floating barrels were exploding into shards of wood meanwhile, encouraged by an equally ferocious bosun, the sailors raced about high above the deck with the dexterity of monkeys within a tree. They expertly navigated the complex web of ropes, cables, and pulleys that formed the running rigging. While the cannons roared below, the rigging crew practiced raising and lowering the various sails and precisely trimming the stretched canvas like one might tune a fine violin. Each small breath of air they extracted from the breezes could mean the difference between life and death in battle. Perfection was their goal and, with trust in their leadership, all labored to the point of exhaustion to exceed their captain's expectations.

While he'd have much preferred to remain on deck to observe the training, Captain Grainger had matters to attend to in his cabin. He had full faith in his leadership team and in his crew's desire to prove their worth as more than mere cadets and children. Grainger opened the door to his cabin to find a groggy prince, roused prematurely from his slumber by the incessant firing of cannons below deck. He wiped the sleep from his eyes and turned to his host. "I swear, if I am asked to wear women's clothing one more time to conceal my identity, I will slit my own throat and order the knife be sent to my father."

"Begging your pardon, your highness," said Captain Grainger, these days somewhat out of practice in the art of hobnobbing with members of the nobility and royal personages, "I'm sure you cannot fault those who were seeking to protect you for they are, at the same time, protecting England herself."

"And I suppose all this yelling and screaming and ear-splitting cannon roaring is meant for my protection, as well?" replied the indignant prince.

It must be said that the first meeting of Prince Rudolph and Captain Grainger was not particularly a cordial one. The prince's foppish reputation preceded him and Grainger was only too aware that Prince Rudolph had been removed from naval service at the request of the Admiralty following alleged amorous escapades with both of an admiral's daughters and, if the rumors were true, their mother, as well. While he had distinguished himself, as it seems, in the art of womanizing, the prince remained a thorn in the side of the royal family. With several older brothers, Rudolph was a little too confident that the distant responsibilities of the crown were unlikely to spoil his rather loose and carefree life of roguery. As such, his primary focus in life became a hedonistic quest for Heaven on Earth. Periodically assigned tasks to demonstrate his noble character, the hapless young man had found countless ways to add upon the disappointment his parents suffered on his account. Prince Rudolph's current mission was no exception. Unconcerned with keeping clandestine affairs of the crown hidden, Rudolph freely described to Captain Grainger how his services had been called upon to secretly meet with rebellion leaders in South America where he might pledge resources and support for their efforts to declare independence from Spain. Somewhere along his journey, his mission was betrayed and Spanish loyalists began the hot pursuit of the fleeing prince. Disguised and transferred from one handler to the next, the prince made his way to Cartagena where he was quietly transferred from a fishing vessel to the awaiting brig, *HMS Conquest*. What he was not aware of was that the Spanish South American fleet had been notified and were scouring the seas for the *Conquest*, a ship whose mission was compromised by a spy within the network. With reliable intelligence, two swift Spanish frigates had been closing the gap for several weeks and had nearly taken their prize. As he told the story of his failed mission, Captain Grainger could see the pain in the prince's eyes. Coming from a long line of respected monarchs, Prince Rudolph had little to show for his time on Earth but for a litany of scandals and an existence of gluttony, intemperance and sloth. For all that, Grainger was not unimpressed with the prince's bold liaisons with rebellion leaders in South America. Sometimes, he thought, a man's worth cannot be fully measured until one allows him to spread his wings and to take that first leap from the fledgling nest into the clear blue sky. While many aspects of the prince's life seemed particularly distasteful to the career seaman, Grainger could not help but pity the young prince, his talents and intellect wasted in the pursuit of pleasure. For all that, the grizzled captain did not intend to play wet nurse to his twenty-seven-year-old passenger, no matter what his lineage.

Days passed and while *HMS Conquest* successfully limped back to Kingston, Jamaica, Grainger worked *HMS Phoebe* along a direct course for Land's End, at the southwestern tip of the English coast, whereupon he would follow the coast to Portsmouth and disembark the prince to the custody of royal guards who would escort the weary traveler back to London.

The officers on the crew successfully stymied speculation about their mysterious guest although the rumors of the captain taking on a mistress to comfort him during his lonely nights were peculiarly amusing to those who knew their captain well enough to know that he typically chose to spend those lonely nights wandering about upon the deck. The unmistakable "clump, clump, clump" of his wooden leg upon the deck told the tale of a man who was more in need of the clean sea air to sustain him than he was of sleep, or mistresses for that matter. His cough worsening by the day, Captain Grainger knew his days were numbered and each moment looking out upon the rolling deep was an invaluable treasure he took not for granted. In the darkness of the night, or beneath the pale moon, his scarred and tormented face was concealed in shadow. Curious eyes, wishing to inspect the battle damage, struggled to avoid the urge to gaze upon their captain's wooden peg leg or at the empty sleeve neatly pinned upon his uniform, across his chest. On deck, his coughs were lost to the wind and muffled by the flapping canvas of the sails, the creaking of the timbers, and the gentle serenade of the sea. In the darkness of the night, no one would spot a tear, infrequent as they may have been.

The sun broke the horizon and greeted a resolute and confident captain. All traces of the frailty that the night had elicited were gone like the morning dew as the new day dawned. It would be a good hour before anyone noticed the sails coming out of the east, hidden before the brilliance of the morning sun.

"*Indomable* and *Fama*, Sir?" asked the stalwart first mate.

Straining to better define the contacts amidst the sparkling waters of the early morning sea, Captain Grainger simply replied, "Mister

Randolph, direct the crew to beat to quarters." And just like that, the ship came to life with men running this way and that, stowing hammocks, preparing the gun deck, and securing all unnecessary items which might become deadly projectiles as the cannon fire wreaked its terrible vengeance. Cadets mustered at their appointed combat stations while the regular crew encouraged them to take heart and be strong.

"Sir, shall we prepare the cannons with round shot, chain, or grapeshot?" asked Lieutenant Carnehall, who had just ascended the ladder from the gun deck. Roundshot could wreak devasting damage upon the hull of an enemy vessel while chainshot was most often used to shred the vulnerable sails or cut the rigging to pieces. When fired, the halves of the ball would separate, a chain extending between the two fragments as it spun toward its target. While typically used against the sails, rigging, or masts of an enemy vessel, if fired across a deck, the spinning chainshot rounds could inflict a terrible toll on the adversary's topside crew, literally cutting sailors and marines in half. Of course, the preferred anti-personnel munition was grapeshot. Grapeshot bags, when fired, dispersed a lethal spray of smaller diameter iron balls. Unfortunately, to get within the reduced range of the grapeshot rounds, Captain Grainger knew he'd have to take *Phoebe* through several full broadsides from the long guns of the more heavily armed *Indomable* and *Fama*. *Phoebe* would likely be battered into submission before she ever closed the distance. Also, as a training vessel with no contingent of royal marines onboard, Captain Grainger knew he would not fare well in a boarding action and thus he had no desire to get too close to either of the enemy frigates, ships no doubt teaming with musket-armed fighters and likely snipers in the tops. It was a French sniper who had taken out Admiral Nelson at the Battle of Trafalgar. Grainger saw his options rapidly falling away.

"Mister Carnehall, move all the guns but for one 18-pounder to the larboard [port] side. Load the guns with round shot, please."

"Sir, all the guns to the larboard side?" asked the second mate, completely bewildered by the unusual request. "Won't she sail awkward in that configuration? We're likely to lose a few knots off our speed."

"To the larboard, Mister Carnehall," replied the captain. The second mate knew only too well that further questioning would not be looked upon kindly and might, on a bad day, see him clapped in irons and escorted below.

Approaching from behind, Lieutenant Randolph handed the captain his telescope. "They're on to us, Sir. We've got the weather gage but we haven't the firepower to drive our point home, I fear."

"Never fear, Jonathan. Fear is an emotion the Admiralty does not sanction and this captain will not tolerate."

"Aye, Captain. 'Never mind maneuvers, always go at them.' Isn't that what Nelson said?"

"Indeed. We can profit from his example—his tactical genius, his courage, and his love of country," replied a stoic Captain Grainger.

With the guns repositioned, Captain Grainger directed his helmsman to set a northerly course. The Spanish frigates, still approaching from the east, turned north, as well, to parallel *Phoebe's* track. Grainger looked over toward his bosun, one of the most seasoned men on the vessel, and, without the question even having to be asked, the bosun shouted out "Making eight knots, down from ten, Captain." As anticipated, *Phoebe's* speed had fallen off with the shifting of the guns to one side. No amount of sail trim could overcome the dramatic shift in the ship's center of gravity. While Captain Grainger fully understood the risk he was taking, the notion of presenting an equal broadside to at least one of the frigates on the larboard side seemed a better option than the two-to-one disadvantage he'd face trying to fight both sides, and then only if he could somehow shake one of the two frigates. The quiet upon the deck was very unsettling to the crew. Running abeam the Spanish frigates, they could tell the Spaniards were slowly edging closer though they lost progress each time they had to tack into the wind to close the lateral distance.

Before the frigates could get within firing range, Captain Grainger directed his crew to unfurl all the sails. "Mainsails, topsails, topgallants, royals, let them all fly!" shouted the captain. With expert precision, sails spread out from every yardarm as cadets and able-bodied seamen flew along the intricate highways of rope, high above the pitching deck. *HMS Phoebe* surged ahead, her masts and lines groaning at the strain—it was all a beautiful chorus to the seasoned ears of the ship's master.

Slow to adjust sails, the Spanish frigates began to fall back. "Twelve knots, Captain," shouted the bosun. Twelve was good...but not good enough. The Spanish heavy frigate, *Indomable*, could not keep pace and grew smaller and smaller in the glasses trained on her from the deck of the *Phoebe*. *Fama*, however, a newer and swifter ship, continued to gain ground, unimpressed by *Phoebe's* spread of sail and expert handling.

"*Indomable's* dropping away, Captain," announced Lieutenant Randolph. "*Fama* is going to leave her and have a go at us by herself."

"And that shall be her undoing," muttered Captain Grainger under his breath.

Both ships continued their race northward, each expertly tacking to try to maximize the advantage of the wind. The sun was setting and *Fama* remained just outside of cannon range...but she was closing the distance, earning each yard of progress with expert seamanship. The officers onboard the *Phoebe* knew what the crew did not; *Fama*, with a trimmer hull and more modern construction, was simply a faster ship and no amount of seamanship was going to negate the end result of the mathematics equation that was playing out before them. An inevitable confrontation with a more powerful vessel was close at hand.

As the sun set, members of the crew each postulated their own theory regarding the captain's plans. Most figured he'd douse the lantern lights and make an unpredictable course change in the hope of losing their pursuer in the darkness. Others thought that, perhaps, he'd try to sneak up on the *Fama* on this moonless night and find a way to disable her. Then there were those excitable youths who dreamed of their captain shouting valiant war cries as he steered directly for the Spanish frigate, confident that God would see to his victory over the Spanish miscreants. They were all wrong. Yet, in some ways, they were all right.

In the dark of the night, *Fama* had given up northerly progress to tack into the wind and earn herself a better position for the next day's fight, upwind from the slower *Phoebe*. Most onboard were not happy to see the Spanish frigate off their larboard stern at sunrise even though she still lagged several miles behind.

The captain went below to his quarters to see if Prince Rudolph would care to join him for breakfast. They were treated to a magnificent meal. Captain Grainger hardly felt it was worth saving the special fare for another day as there remained a distinct possibility that he might not live to see it. Toward the end of the meal, he asked that his steward bring forward his finest bottle of wine. Captain Grainger poured a glass for himself and for the prince. Raising his glass, he proposed a toast...but not to England, or the king, not to God or the angels above, not even to the brave men of the *Phoebe* for whom he held responsibility, each of their lives dependent upon his judgment and decisions. "To redemption!" he exclaimed. Prince Rudolph, taken aback but noticeably moved, clinked his glass against Captain Grainger's.

"To redemption."

With the meal complete, Captain Grainger handed the bottle with its remaining wine to his steward and asked that he share it with the crew when the victory had been won. His steward, fanatically loyal to his captain, acknowledged without the slightest pause or indication of doubt.

Back upon deck, *Fama* was drawing noticeably closer and was beginning to fire ranging shots from its brass bow chaser guns. The balls were splashing short of *Phoebe's* stern but Captain Grainger knew that, within the hour, his ship would be vulnerable to his foe's long guns.

Captain Grainger made his rounds throughout the ship, encouraging his men and shaking each hand, individually. He felt incredibly proud of the progress his young crew had made and he felt honored to serve beside each and every one. He made one last stop in his cabin to advise the prince on the safest place to shelter during what was sure to be a brutal battle. The prince was gone. The captain's steward, stowing the breakfast table, and especially the glassware, said that the prince had left the cabin with a determined look on his face, his fine rapier seated in the scabbard affixed to his sword belt.

"Well, at least we'll have one for the boarding party," joked Captain

Grainger, who was inwardly inspired by the prince's desire to contribute to what might well be a losing battle.

"Two, Sir," replied the steward, holding up one of the captain's elegant dinner knives.

"That's the spirit, Brickney! Rule Britannia!"

Standing amidst his officers in quiet repose, Captain Grainger seemed to be waiting for some indeterminate point in time or space that only he could identify. One of *Fama's* bow chaser rounds thudded against *Phoebe's* stern but did little apparent damage. It wasn't the 12-pounder chase guns that concerned the captain. Judging the distances and relative speeds of the two vessels, Captain Grainger made his move.

"Helmsman, hard a larboard!" he shouted. The ship rapidly turned toward the left, the added weight of the guns on the larboard side made for an even nimbler maneuver in that direction.

Several of the more seasoned crew members explained to the cadets that the captain was maneuvering to "Cross the T." In doing so, placing the ships perpendicular to each other, the ship with its broadside facing the bow or stern of its adversary had a daunting advantage with respect to how much firepower it could bring to bear. Beyond that, a broadside of grapeshot along the entire length of the adversary's deck could potentially decimate a crew. Roundshot was loaded as it was the enemy's ship, more than its crew, that Captain Grainger hoped to cripple.

"Mister Randolph, takeover topside. I'm going below to the gun deck," said the captain.

"Aye aye, Captain. Take this fight too those bastards, Sir!"

Grainger hurried toward the ladder, stumbling as he went and frustrated that he could no longer race between fighting positions as he had during his youth. He all but fell to the deck below but refused help from a gunner's mate.

The *Fama*, fully expecting *Phoebe* to strike her colors and surrender, was completely caught off guard when the English frigate rapidly changed course and was about to bring the full weight of her broadside against her nearly undefended bow. With the ships momentum carrying it rapidly into firing range, there was little *Fama* could do beyond bracing for the barrage. Although she only had 17 guns trained at the *Fama*, the now proficient crew of the *Phoebe*, fighting like true veterans, fired them with devasting effect, several rounds penetrating the hull below the waterline so that the Spanish frigate began to rapidly take on water. As if posing for his statue, Prince Rudolph waved his sword in the air, encouraging the gun crews to reload as the truth about his identity spread like wildfire throughout the ship. "It's the Prince! The prince is fighting alongside us, boys! Rally for Prince Rudolph and for Captain Grainger!"

Despite their best efforts, the crew was unable to get off another broadside before both vessels' momentum carried them along their paths, now putting *Phoebe's* exposed stern at risk as *Fama* slipped behind her. Looking to maximize damage to the English ship's crew, *Fama* had loaded all her cannons with grapeshot and intended to rake her adversary's deck with the deadly spray of small iron balls. Topside, Lieutenant Randolph directed all deck hands to lay flat, anticipating the shotgun-like spray from the grapeshot rounds. Fortunately for the crew of HMS *Phoebe*, the absence of half her guns contributed to her sitting high in the water. Rather than sweeping across the deck, killing sailors, the grapeshot rounds largely bounced off the stern, the primary casualty being the captain's dinnerware which had been secured in the stern gallery.

As *Fama* passed beyond the stern of the *Phoebe*, Captain Grainger shouted out to relay a message to the helmsman to turn hard to starboard so that the single 18-pounder cannon on that side might come to bare upon the stern of the *Fama* before she could turn to fire another full broadside against the *Phoebe*. The captain peered anxiously through the gunport. With the weight of all the guns on the larboard side, HMS *Phoebe* was not turning as efficiently to starboard. This was a perilous and pivotal moment in the engagement. On deck, Lieutenant Randolph was ordering a reduction in sail, knowing full well that any improvement in turn radius might mean the difference between life and death. On the gundeck, Grainger moved behind the cannon and stared down the sights. His one chance to gain the upper hand in the engagement, he thought, was to strike and disable the *Fama's* rudder, thus rendering her unsteerable. The bow of the *Fama* came into view and he could tell they were, likewise, turning hard to attempt to parallel *Phoebe's* heading. While the odds were not in *Phoebe's* favor, Captain Grainger felt that he, and he alone, should carry the responsibility for firing the win-or-lose round that was packed into the gun. Before he could realize his destiny, two shots from the *Fama's* stern chaser cannons, aimed to disable the single gun protruding from *Phoebe's* starboard gundeck, penetrated the hull and sent a deadly spray of splintered wood flying through the tight confines of the deck. Amidst the dust and debris, confusion reigned. Prince Rudolph, knocked off his feet, could see the captain laying on his back, his remaining leg shattered and bleeding profusely. A medical officer ran over to attend Captain Grainger but he spit and cursed and crawled back toward the cannon, falling forward, flat on his chest, several times. Despite his pain, Grainger would not be dissuaded from his return to the cannon. As he pulled himself up, he felt a hand upon his shoulder. Looking back, he saw the determined face of Prince Rudolph.

"Captain Grainger, if you please," said the prince, "I was a fairly accomplished gunner during my time in the Royal Navy if not a particularly notable officer. I beg you afford me the opportunity for this one parting shot, a chance at redemption, if you will, as I'm sure neither God nor king shall afford me another opportunity such as this should I live to be a hundred."

Time was of the essence and it would be wrong to say that Captain Grainger considered the request as there was no time left for calculations and assessments. Instinctively, he slid off to the side of the cannon and permitted the prince to sight in the gun, raising its elevation ever so slightly to account for the distance to the target. Taking the wind speed into account, and a fraction of a second before *Fama's* rudder was aligned with the axis of the gun barrel, Prince Rudolph adeptly slid to the right side of the cannon to be clear of the 5,000-pound weapon's recoil, and then ignited the powder in the touch hole with a slow match he had been holding. With a thunderous roar, the cannon launched its 18-pound ball of iron at 1,700 feet per second, enveloping the area in a giant cloud of smoke. From the gundeck, nothing was visible initially. A rousing cheer from topside was the confirmation that the crew's prayers had been answered. As winds cleared the smoke from the area, Grainger and Prince Rudolph both peered out the gun port to see the *Fama*, now rudderless, sailing away. Instinctively, Lieutenant Randolph turned the *Phoebe* away from the treat. When word came from below that the captain was seriously injured, he passed control of the vessel over to the second mate, Lieutenant Carnehall, and slide down the ladder to the gundeck to attend to his captain. Below deck, Lieutenant Randolph was startled to see Captain Grainger, propped up against the side of the cannon, sitting in a pool of his own blood. More surprising still, the captain was laughing—something Jonathan Randolph had convinced himself that Captain Grainger was physically incapable of doing. He could not help but laugh, too, as he knelt to assess the damage to Captain Grainger's leg. Moments later, the ships surgeon arrived at the scene. The grave expression on his face told the first mate more than any voiced medical opinion could have. Randolph grasped Captain Grainger's hand and held it tightly. "Doctor Winston will have you patched up and sea worthy in no time, Captain," said the first mate, a comforting smile on his face.

"You are, by far, the worst liar I have ever met, Jonathan," chided Captain Grainger, with true affection in his voice. "Bring *Phoebe* home and pray we might both see England's green coast together one last time."

Prince Rudolph, still high from the adrenalin rush of the engagement, turned to Captain Grainger as the surgeon supervised his transfer to a canvas stretcher to be taken to the surgeon's operating table. "But Captain, now that we've disabled those Spanish villains, aren't we going to finish them off?"

"Those aren't our orders, your highness. Had we a larger crew, we might capture her and bring her back home for England's glory. Alas, we have barely enough young lads onboard to keep *Phoebe* sailing straight and true. Besides, the Spanish captain handled his ship magnificently and with honor. Poseidon himself might revolt against us should we pound the Spanish ship until it sunk to the depths with all hands lost. No, that simply wouldn't do." Captain Grainger paused to cough several times, the nature of his coughing only serving to further alarm the attending doctor. "The Spanish captain shall live to sail another day but if he's wise, he'll steer well clear of any Royal Navy ships in the years to come."

"It's a noble and charitable judgment you levy, to be sure, Captain Grainger," said the prince. I'd swear to it that this Spanish rascal captain has never before nor will ever again meet the likes of you--a commander and a seaman of inestimable ingenuity and skill." Not to be won over by any manner of praise, and humble to the core, the captain simply nodded, graciously. Prince Rudolph stepped back to allow the sailors carrying the stretcher to move past.

Lieutenant Randolph found the opportunity to improve upon his lying skills as HMS *Phoebe* steadily made progress toward the coast of England. He assured the young crew that their captain was well and enjoying some much-needed rest along with a respectable quantity of fine French wine which he had previously convinced a French merchant vessel to part with. The more seasoned crewmembers were not so easily deceived as they could read an officer's lies much as a hawk reads a hare. All felt somewhat relieved when, shortly after the welcomed cry of "Land Ho!" rang out, they saw Captain Grainger, assisted by Prince Rudolph, make an appearance on deck to enjoy the view of their beloved English coastline. A few of the younger boys gasped, seeing that the lower half of what was previously Captain Grainger's good leg was now conspicuously absent. The surgeon had to amputate the limb to save the captain's life. He now steadied himself with two crutches aided, in no small part, by the prince who helped ensure the motion of the pitching ship would not topple the heroic naval hero.

In due course, following the southern coastline of England and now in familiar waters, HMS *Phoebe* arrived at her appointed destination, Portsmouth. The previous evening, all the officers joined the captain and Prince Rudolph for a final dinner, the likes of which would have made the king, himself, envious.

In port, appropriate liaisons were made and arrangements finalized for the royal escorts to receive Prince Rudolph for his return journey, by carriage, to London. Before permitting his guest to disembark, Captain Grainger asked Prince Rudolph if he might be willing to deliver a personal letter to the king, on his behalf. Ever-grateful, the prince willingly agreed to deliver the sealed missive. With the warmest of farewells, the royal and the sailor parted ways. Despite the prince's pleas, Captain Grainger graciously declined the offer to accompany Prince Rudolph to London where he might then be treated by the best physicians in all of England. Grainger said he had some pressing matters to attend to that simply could not wait. He spoke the truth.

In London, Prince Rudolph described the great gallantry of Captain Grainger and crew and he was hardly through his story before the gathered nobles were pledging their wealth to erect a marble statue to honor the great man. All of Captain Grainger's past transgressions, perceived or actual, were quickly forgotten and completely forgiven. In the telling of this great saga, Prince Rudolph humbly understated his own actions. The true nature of his contribution was revealed upon the opening of the sealed letter Captain Grainger had entrusted to the prince's care. The king beamed with pride. Rudolph's siblings, as many who were there to hear the king's courtier read the letter aloud, were astonished to learn of the gallant actions of their much-maligned brother. None would look upon the prince in the same way again and the prestige the young prince earned further inspired him to improve upon his character and to live with honor and integrity.

It is with honor and integrity that Captain Jonathan Grainger had lived his life. He regained his status amidst the great sailors in British history and naval students, for generations to come, would learn of his great skill upon the sea in defense of their nation. A large statue was, in fact, placed within a central square to commemorate his deeds. While members of the nobility suggested that his body might, one day, be entombed beside that of Horatio Viscount Nelson, beneath the dome of St. Paul's Cathedral, the truth of the matter is that the good captain had other plans. Prince Rudolph had not yet completed his return to London before Captain Grainger, having successfully completed his duty, rendered his final salute to the men of *HMS Phoebe* before returning to his cabin to peacefully plot his course into the uncharted waters of the Great Beyond. *HMS Phoebe* made her way along the coast, on a westerly heading, as the seas began to churn, a great storm approaching.

Off the coast of Falmouth, *HMS Phoebe* dropped anchor. "You know, Andrew," said a pensive Jonathan Randolph, "this is where Captain Grainger first learned to sail. He was born just over there, beyond that cluster of lighted cottages. He loved the sea beyond measure and, like with so many of us, he could not deny its calling."

"He served England well, Sir, as well as any man could."

"As well as most, to be sure, Andrew. Are you ready then?"

"Aye, Captain," replied Lieutenant Carnehall.

The first mate, Lieutenant Andrew Carnehall, signaled to the gathered sailors who then carefully slid the sailcloth-encased body of their former captain over the side of the ship. Thunder crashed above and lightning flashed in the sky as the cannon balls, sewn into the sailcloth of the burial covering, carried the body beneath the waves.

"Me thinks the angels are greeting our beloved captain with a fine broadside salute," said a tearful Captain Randolph. Lieutenant Carnehall, listening to the thunder roaring above, could not help but agree.

"That they are, Sir. That they are."

SEA OF HEARTBREAK

WILLIAM JOHN ROSTRON

Seasick? Yeah, I understand the concept because of that one disastrous cruise we took. My understanding was further intensified by my inability to make it from Long Island to Connecticut on the ferry without any physical reaction. Seasick—I understand it. What I don't understand is feeling it while sitting in my den staring at my computer!

Perhaps there is a connection—seasick and computer? After all, I am busy reconstructing my family tree on Ancestry.com and oddly finding generations of sailors. Before the woozy stomach developed, I almost started singing Jimmy Buffet's "Son of a Son of a Sailor." Ironically, the words seem ridiculous. "The seas in my veins, my tradition remains." So what's that all about?

It's not that I don't love the sea, especially since I live on a Long *Island*. The water is all around me, and there are hundreds of miles of beaches. That's just how I like my saltwater...around me—while I sit on my butt in the sand looking out at it. I like to see the sea—just not be *on* it.

Back to my dilemma of seasickness. It started when I located my father's World War II records. He was in the navy for six years, stationed on an LST heading for the possible invasion of the Japanese mainland. Those LST ships had front ends that opened up and allowed the attacking soldiers and armaments to charge the beach directly. I think that LST stood for something about that function. However, I remember my father telling me that the sailors all believed it stood for long, slow target. With the massive troop total on board, many of these ships were the focus of the Japanese navy and air force. Far too many of the LSTs were sunk by these forces.

That's how far I got in my research when the seasickness prevailed. While staring at the records, I started to see white. Then, I had some stomach pain, and the world got blurry.

While I understand that you may want to have me committed once you hear my story, I will relate what happened next anyway. First, I started to hallucinate (a new seasick symptom indeed). Then, I found myself actually *on* the LST! Japanese planes were diving the ship and wreaking havoc on its deck. Meanwhile, I could discern at least one submarine in the distance waiting to unload a torpedo. Casualties were being taken on board, so I ignored my seasickness, embarrassed that my minor foible even existed in light of these injured sailors.

I wondered how the ship would hold out against this barrage. More selfishly, how would it affect me? Though no one noticed me, I felt like I was there. It was not like a dream or even a hallucination anymore.

Then in the air, I heard a new sound…a different sound. I knew before looking up that this was the hum of American planes coming to the rescue. They fought the Japanese Zeroes to a standstill, and the enemy eventually disengaged, and the submarine likewise fled in the face of attack.

As I looked around, I saw the carnage the attack had wrought. However, there was nothing to impede the ship's mission or even slow down its speed. The only price paid had been in human lives, and the surviving sailors reverently attended to those bodies.

The wounded all streamed in the same direction, which I assumed contained the sickbay. I followed. There, I found organized chaos. The doctors were overwhelmed with severe injuries while their assistants triaged the wounded, deciding to send them on to surgery or bandage them. While looking at these assistants, I drew back in shock. I should have known. I should have understood then why I was in this illusion, this hallucination, this dream…whatever the hell it was. I saw a pair of hands nimbly and expertly stitching and bandaging a shrapnel wound. The *same hands* that would place a bandage on *my* cuts and bruises a decade later. As I stared at the name tag on his uniform, I realized that five years later, I would be born and given this same name, with a "Junior" appendage at the end. I could swear he looked up from his mission and smiled at me. But that couldn't be…

I was back at my computer, the seasickness subsiding rapidly. Dare I go on? I never knew or met my paternal grandfather and had no knowledge of his life. However, he was next on my research list. I trembled as I considered the possibilities into which I could be drawn. Imagine if this relative was something less desirable, like a gangster or a serial killer. Would I enter into that world with my "seasickness?"

The only mention of my grandfather that I had ever heard was that he abandoned the family in 1930. My father was eight at the time. My grandparents and my father moved to New York so that my grandfather could seek employment in the merchant marine. That was the last time anyone mentioned his name. "Fred" had essentially disappeared from the human race as far I or anyone related to me knew. Now it was my job to solve the mystery.

I don't know which came first, "the seasickness" or the astonishment of what I found. At first, it was a simple internet find…Fred had worked on a ship heading from New York to Amsterdam. So, he was trying to earn a living in the depression. But why did he never come back to his family? As the documents revealed the course of his life, it became evident that he may not have done right by his family, he was indeed a brave and heroic man. Between 1930 and 1955, he made 37 Atlantic crossings. This included trips from 1939 to 1945…while German wolfpack submarines tried to sink every ship bringing American goods into Europe to aid the war effort. These unarmed ships were sitting targets for the Nazi predators in many cases. However, the merchant marine job was as necessary as any in the armed forces. I realized that unbeknownst to each other, both my father and grandfather were on the seas doing important work at the same time…in two different oceans.

I should have expected the "seasickness" to afflict me at that point, but I still was caught by surprise when it did.

The slow, lumbering vessel I found myself on seemed almost deserted. I peered through a porthole to see most of the crew engaged in dinner. I was immediately thankful that there were no diving-bombing planes or menacing submarines. I walked the deck, keeping close to the railing in case I felt the need to upchuck my last meal.

Eventually, I saw two sailors on watch while the others ate their meal. One appeared extremely young and, if I judged correctly, somewhat frightened. The other looked to be in his late forties—just the age my grandfather would have been in 1944. It had to be him, or why would my "seasickness" have brought me here? I approached them. Like my experience on the LST, I did not seem to be visible to them.

"Fred, I damn afraid. I got a wife and kid home, and I wouldn't have signed on if I didn't need the money for them. I keep thinking that there's going to be a torpedo on the horizon and that we're all going to die in this forsaken North Atlantic graveyard."

"You can't be thinking that way," declared the older man, Fred, who I assumed was my long-lost grandfather."

"Why the hell not?"

"I've made this trip thirteen times each way...and I'm still here."

"For how long? I was just listening to a couple of officers talking. Us merchant marine guys have a higher death rate than the guys in the army or the navy. It's just a matter of time. Maybe I should have joined the army instead."

I was drawn closer. No one had ever mentioned that it was more dangerous to be in the merchant marine than in the army. I am a history buff, and I had never heard that tidbit of reality. Now Fred stared down at the young man and thought carefully before speaking.

"You don't want to be doing that," whispered Fred, his thoughts intensely swirling in his head.

"Why not? What do you know about the army? You been on this ship for the entire war?"

"This one."

"What's that mean?"

"Dammit, don't you young folk study history in school anymore?

Exactly thirty years ago, the same countries were in a war…France, Germany, England, and eventually the U.S."

"You didn't…."

"Yes, I did. I signed up as soon as I was old enough. And I wasn't even an American citizen. My family had come to the United States in 1911 from England. I became of age just as our country joined the war."

"But you look fine. You survived."

"Yeah, but I was only there a few months before it ended. It was enough time to see what hell really was. The mustard gas, the trenches, the land mines…the sheer carnage."

"But you did come home to your family alive."

"*I* did."

The way he emphasized the "I," I knew there was much more to my grandfather Fred's story. I moved in closer because I could feel that this was what I was doing here. I needed to know what he was going to tell the young man.

"The war started in 1914, but not for America. My family had just come from England three years before, and so my older brothers felt a duty to join the fight when the country of our birth immediately entered the war. My older brother John immediately sailed for England and joined their army in an elite group known as the Hussars. Unfortunately, he was wounded in his leg. When he recovered, he was sent back to the front lines, where he was again shot in the leg. This time he lost that limb."

"I can see…."

"No, you can't! My brother Harry turned 18 in 1916. He couldn't get to England because of the submarines, and America was still not in the war. So Harry joined the Canadian army. They knew how to evade the submarines well enough for him to get their troops across the Atlantic safely."

"Did Harry make it?"

"Yes and No. At the battle of Vimy Ridge, his unit ran head-on into a gas attack. Harry's lungs were so damaged that he still could not breathe right even after being hospitalized for two years. Like my brother John, he was an invalid for the rest of his life. They are both gone now."

I cried at the story of my two great-uncles. But, I knew this story was at an end. Fred spoke one last time.

"Look out there as far as you can see... what's there?"

"Water."

"Right. It may not be everyone's choice, but I will always choose the sea."

"What do you mean?"

"We're in a God-forsaken war. We could be victims...just like John and Harry. But I don't want to live being carried around by my friends and relatives. Or not able to breathe well enough even to take a walk with my children. Out here, if we are attacked, either we live or die... there is no in between. That's the way I want it.

I understood or thought I understood why my grandfather never returned to his wife or child. As irrational as it may seem to me, or most people, he never wanted to leave the sea.

It would be all or nothing.

I was back at my computer with the remnants of watery eyes from Grandfather Fred's story still drying. I think that I had had enough geneology/seasickness for a lifetime. I was looking forward to hanging out with the actual living people who made up my close-knit group. Would I tell them of my experience? Probably not. Not if I want to keep living in my home and not some institution complete with a straight jacket.

As I am about to shut down all the programs running on my Mac, I see the familiar leaf on the Ancestry program. That means they had found a connection that, before now, had been hidden. Should I click on it? Just one more time?

The cold water pierces my skin. Hypothermia is rapidly setting in. Another hallucination? An illusion? A dream? No, the water is too, too cold for that. I cannot even feel the seasickness because I am so numb that I feel nothing. Can I die in this make-believe world? I try to find a reason for my imminent demise but can't. My English ancestors came over by ship in 1911 without incident. My Italian ancestors made the trip ten years before that date without any significant problems.

I look around for clues as if knowing the why of my situation will help out. Hundreds of drowned or frozen bodies float in the water around me. I now feel sick to my stomach, but with the self-absorbent seasickness of before, but rather with revulsion for what I am witnessing around me.

I see a ship in the distance…sinking. Did I jump from its deck? If so, it could not have been long ago, or I would be dead or make-believe dead. Who knows? My last vivid thought is no wonder I hate ships and the ocean.

Consciousness is leaving me as I see what looks like a lifeboat heading my way. Wait! Can they see me? An arm reaches out to pull me into the half-empty boat. As my sides scrap the oar holders, I start to bleed. I don't care. I am in the lifeboat and safe. Why is this experience different than the others. Perhaps because I didn't find my ancestor? Maybe he or she will find me?

I hear loud explosions, and everyone in my rescue craft gasps…and screams…and cries. The ship…their ship…my ship(?) is going down. The others have wrapped a blanket around me, and I am content to sit quietly. Yet, my curiosity is overwhelming. If I watch the ship go down, will my dream end? But I have seen no relative! No genealogical reason for my near death.

"They said this couldn't happen," shrieks an inconsolable woman. I hear other people in other boats screaming in a cacophony of distress and terror. Yet I am most moved by the woman next to me who simply murmurs, "God rest their souls."

I can not resist any longer. I look…just in time to see the stern rushing to join the rest of the ship in its watery grave. The victims remaining on board are now jumping into the vortex created by the rapidly sinking ship. My eyes fix on one singular tragic figure as he plunges passed the word "Titanic."

This is crazy. No one in my family was on the Titanic. No one even knew anyone on that doomed vessel. How do I know this? I am still here. Safe but freezing on this lifeboat in the frigid North Atlantic. Why?

It seems like days, but it is really only hours that we float on the lonely frozen sea before seeing lights in the distance. I know some of the history of the tragic event in which I now find myself involved. The sinking Titanic contacted many ships, and most did not respond for fear of the very iceberg that had punctured the side of the "unsink-able" ship. Only one vessel responded to rescue those set adrift. It must be the HMS Carpathia in the distance.

I remember reading at age ten the Walter Lord book, *A Night to Remember*, and being struck by something interesting in the true story of the sinking of the Titanic. However, all details of that book were washed away by the Hollywood blockbuster movie of the same name. The epic rewrote the history of the Titanic, and all I can see and remember are Leonardo DeCaprio and Kate Winslet...and the bodies floating in the water. They got that part right.

The Carpathia closes in on us. The rowboats flock to her light like moths to a flame, a flame of promised warmth and safety. Our turn comes soon, and I climb the ropes to the waiting deck. Real hands touch me and assist me to a spot on the deck where I am given more blankets, food, and water. The crew works tirelessly under the direc-tion of one man who is seeing to every detail of the rescue. As he personally ministers to many of the disheveled, starving survivors, his voice is never silent with commands to others to do likewise. And then he passes me by. He stops...looks back at me for a split second...and smiles. He is then on his way.

Who is he? I stop a crew member passing by, point at the leader, and ask that question. He laughs.

"You'd never know it, but that is our captain...Capt. Arthur Henry Rostron."

Now I remember why I found the book, *A Night to Remember*, so interesting six decades ago. The captain of the Carpathia and I shared the same uncommon last name. I knew why I was here.

Immediately, I found myself sitting at the computer—all the phys-ical ailments I had had only moments before were gone. I walked over to a bookshelf where I kept all the volumes I had read in my life that I had found fascinating for one reason or another. I took *A Night to Remember* off the shelf and quickly leafed through the pages to the center of the book, where there were photographs. One caption read, "Captain Arthur Henry Rostron of the Carpathia. Responsible for the rescue of all of the survivors of the Titanic." I saw the resemblance.

Though this is a work of fiction, author William John Rostron is related to Chief Petty Officer William John Rostron, Sr. (LST)...Fred Rostron (merchant marine and American Expeditionary Force, WWI)...John Rostron, Her Majesty's Hussars, WWI...Harry Rostron, Canadian Army, WWI...and Sir Arthur Henry Rostron, Captain of the Carpathia.

MARINA RISING

ELAINE DONADIO

Submerged, rhythmically undulating with the cadence of crashing waves, I glide from trough to crest, riding the billowing foam, a bucking bronco, unrelenting in its quest to dispossess the stubborn interloper in this boundless realm. Undeterred, I forge ahead with my wild ride, following the jagged coastline, avoiding the craggy rocks, envying access to the cliff-tops and sand dunes, domain of the land dwellers. I spy a lone young woman precariously stepping across the rocks. She is unsteady, but I still envy her freedom.

By the ethereal glow of the full moon, night shadows are cast along Cliff Walk, the scenic overlook from the Forty Steps to the luxurious *cottages* luring the multitudes to this island that is really not an island at all. Boutique hotels, trendy restaurants, historical cemeteries, tales of hauntings and sea monsters, embellished by the lure of sunken ships abound with treasure, neon lights beckoning visitors to this haven connecting Narragansett Bay to Rhode Island Sound and the vast Atlantic Ocean.

Although I am cognizant of the dangers, I am a frequent visitor to this rugged shoreline. I slink in the depths and shadows of this seemingly infinite realm. I am quick and clever but still exercise constant vigilance to escape capture. Yes, it is true that I am a shape shifter and can count on creatures of the sea to help me if I find myself in danger, but I do not wish to put this to the test. Life in this vast ocean presents enough challenges without tempting Fate.

And, yet ... here I am, sometimes in plain sight. English is not my first language. I have honed my telegraphic powers to learn the language of the two-legged terrestrial mammals. Sound is amplified over the water, giving me the opportunity to eavesdrop on conversations of the land dwellers. When I hear the words, my power of mental telepathy allows me to understand and communicate. My parents are the esteemed leaders of my world. As their only child, it is expected that I should be both fearless and wise. It is inevitable that I should explore this world and share information and knowledge with the other Merfolk. I am told that I will know when it is my time to reign. It will become clear to me when it is time to take decisive action that will exert positive influence on our world.

"Help! Help!" I hear the terrified screams. I look for the young woman on the cliff, but she is not there. Realizing she has lost her footing, I race to the sound of her voice, grabbing her by the hips, pushing her upward toward the shoreline. She coughs up the swallowed water, then looks around. Puzzled, she cries out, "Who's out there? Where are you?"

Through the powers of my mind, I convey my message, "You are safe now. Go."

She does not give up, "You're scaring me. Is this some kind of joke?" When she receives no answer, she runs away, frequently looking over her shoulder.

I am careful not to be seen. I am not ready to reveal myself.

Mermaids are spiritual beings, known for our enchanting songs and our magical, prophetic powers. We bathe in the light of the full moon to strengthen our mystical connections. The moonstone is the symbol of divine feminine energy that is directly connected to the waxing and waning of the moon. Mermaids are not to be confused with Sirens that harbor negativity and malice. Mermaids are benevolent. We enjoy synergistic relationships with dolphins, whales, and octopuses and often work together to try to save humans in danger of drowning. Sailors of old were always happy to see mermaids—they knew dolphins would be nearby to chase the sharks away from the ships.

Is it so far-fetched to believe that life branched off into a marine environment as well as terra firma? In the quest for food and the need to escape aggressive land animals, Merfolk took to the oceans. As our bodies adapted to marine life we lived in harmony with most creatures in the unexplored depths and easily communicated with them. Our first sounds consist mostly of clicks and whistles so we can easily communicate with dolphins and whales, sharing a natural affinity. As we grow older, our gills form vocal cords allowing us to communicate with one another in Mermish. If the occasional shark forgets the unwritten rule of the deep, or humans get too close for comfort, we can quickly call for help from the highly intelligent and resourceful dolphins and octopuses. The neighboring Cetaceans are never too far away to create a diversion. Or, we can count on the nearby octopus to create a camouflage screen with its black ink, allowing us time to change our shape into a much less interesting plant or sea creature or to slip unnoticed into another dimension of time and space.

"Where are you? I know you're out there." The young woman has returned with a rowdy group of friends —splashing and pushing one another—frolicking in the shallows. "I don't know who or what you are, but this isn't funny."

"Hey, maybe it was a sea monster. *Grrrowl!*" A burly young man throws his beer can into the waves.

"Don't do that, you idiot! Why do you have to throw trash in the ocean?"

"Avalyn, lighten up. One bottle in this big ocean won't make a difference."

"Just stop fooling around and help me figure out what it was."

"It was probably the ghost of some crazy sea captain. *Booo!*" a second young man teases. "On target!" He throws the plastic six-pack ringed beer holder, successfully encircling the bobbing beer can.

"Stop it! Don't you have any respect?" Avalyn chides.

"Chillax," he answers.

"I think you imagined the whole thing. Almost drowning can do that to people. It's normal," a young woman with sprayed purple hair tries to comfort Avalyn.

"You're all wrong. She saved me and I understood her message even though I didn't hear words."

The young men laughed at this revelation.

"Too much tequila!" one shouted.

"Better watch out! It's alien mind control!" another one teased.

"Avalyn, you didn't see anything then and there's nothing here now," purple hair tries to take the edge off. "What you're describing doesn't sound believable."

"But, still ..."

I am happy when the group finally leaves. I feel a concordance with Avalyn as my mind churns with ideas for possible opportunities. I sense she is a kindred spirit. If she returns, my hopes may see fruition.

I hear the unmistakable sounds of a baby dolphin swimming toward the shore—alarming that it is separated from its mother. I immediately search for the offending trash but only find the beer can. Before I know it, the calf is gone and so is the plastic six-pack ring. I am concerned. Floating objects become toys for young sea mammals. They'll put their snouts through the rings and toss them or swim with them on the tips of their snouts. The problem is they don't have arms to remove them, so the plastic stays with them forever. Hoping the mother has been reunited with her calf, I click a warning of the possible danger. I do not hear any response. I call to the calf, but no answer

My mind wanders to my memories of this unique corner of the world. The waters around Newport, Rhode Island are filled with tales of ghosts, sea monsters, and tragedies. The sea hides its secrets well. The ocean floor, devoid of light except for the soft glow provided by biofluorescent and bioluminescent sea creatures that break up the blackness, is a bleak graveyard to thousands of ships dashed against rocks, overturned by an angry and unpredictable sea, or blown apart by exploding armaments. Remnants of lives once lived and dreams unfulfilled, many lost in gaping chasms that attract human divers filled with awe and wonder or the promise of lost treasure.

Bulls-eye! Burnt bodies. Drownings! The Battle of Point Judith, May

1945. A German U-boat sank an American coal collier, *Black Point*, killing many. Attracted by the noise of the explosion, I propelled as many as I could to the surface. I whistled and clicked for dolphins to come to disperse the circling sharks. We could not save everyone. The next day, the American Navy retaliated against their enemy. I watched helplessly as the boat sank to the bottom. I swam around the wreckage hoping for some survivors to make their way through the hatch. The escape portal never opened. I tried in vain to open it. All hands were lost—entombed in an underwater ship of war.

This haunted site is now designated as a war grave. Divers are forbidden to remove artifacts. Braving underwater cliffs and passages, the enormous stacked boulders created thousands of years ago by shifting glaciers, divers continue to explore the dangerous wreck, some giving their lives in their quest for adventure. I do what I can to buoy divers overcome by embolisms or cardiac and respiratory issues. Good intentions are not always enough.

Northeast towards Newfoundland, on April 14, 1912, the whales' message of disaster reverberated through the dark waters of the North Atlantic, broadcasting news of the of sinking of the *RMS Titanic*, the luxury steamship on its maiden voyage, taking at least 1,500 of its 2,240 passengers and crew to their watery grave. The lucky ones boarded lifeboats to be picked up by the nearby RMS Carpathia during the night. Others were not so blessed. Groups of Merfolk, dolphins and giant octopuses surrounded the hapless victims in the icy water.

We worked in concert to procure debris to be used as flotation devices—beams, door, furniture, wood paneling, and cork from the bulkheads—after the ship broke into two parts. The giant octopuses used their long suctioned-cupped arms to carry as many passengers as possible to the surface. But many writhed free in terror, more afraid of the huge cephalopods than the dangers of the deep. While whales continued to broadcast their pleas for help, we plunged into the depths to bring those lifesavers to the terrified humans as they either jumped or were thrown into the gloomy blackness. Sadly, they could not be saved from the effects of the icy water. Hypothermia set in. Their systems shut down as their fingers were permanently bent in a hold-on-for-dear-life fruitless clutch. Their vacant eyes searched for rescue. All dead within the hour. There was nothing more we could do.

Would-be divers are disappointed to learn that it is impossible to explore the wreck of the Titanic without specialized equipment. SCUBA equipment is not sufficient at such depths. It wasn't until 1985 that the first scientific expedition was prepared for such a quest. I have overheard divers speaking of the importance of Google Earth in determining the location of this ill-fated ship. Coordinates 41.7325° N, 49.9469° W. While artifacts have been found—shoes and a hand mirror —there are no remains of the victims—no bodies, skeletons, or clothing. The flesh was most likely eaten by ravenous sea creatures and the skeletons dissolved by the caustic sea salt. Hanging icicle-like growths called *rusticles* provide visual evidence of the bacteria eating away at the hull. It is believed that all evidence of the wreck will be completely erased by the year 2030. The iconic Titanic will exist no more.

I have communicated this information to the fish, crabs and corals using this ship as a habitat. Perhaps the corals will continue to branch out, building their vertical wall as an independent ecosystem. Their importance must not be diminished. Throughout the world, corals are known as the *Rainforest of the Sea*. They provide the foundation for underwater life: sheltering sea creatures, filtering water, protecting coastlines from erosion and flooding, producing oxygen for sea life, and cleaning the atmosphere. Most importantly, corals are not rocks or plants, but are living breathing simple animals, found across the world's oceans in both shallow and deep water, with tremendous responsibility in supporting the balance of nature.

I fear that human disregard and carelessness will continue to adversely affect oceans and ocean life. Marine debris from garbage dumping leads to choking, suffocating, entangling and killing of marine life. Wasteful over-fishing with miles-long nets depletes resources and food supplies and kills many unintended catch callously labeled as collateral damage. Swimmers often use sunscreen products that are harmful to coral reef habitats. Dumping of toxic chemicals changes the oxygen composition necessary for the health of all sea life.

Divers can deliberately or inadvertently break off fragile coral branches that should never be touched in any way. Kicking up sand or sediment by over-finning can block sunlight needed by algae (photosynthesis), the food source of corals.

Noise pollution also presents extreme dangers to marine mammals and other sea creatures that use echolocation and sonar to communicate location of food sources and nearby danger, migration patterns, and homing signals to lost members of the pods. Narragansett Bay is best known as a summer recreational retreat for many wealthy people, but it is also a testing ground for the US Navy Undersea Warfare Center where underwater self-propelled drones emit signals. Combined with production and testing of underwater weapons, vehicles, acoustic sensor equipment and transmission systems, these modern technological advances corrupt and interfere with communication, navigation and echolocation of many marine mammals.

Noise from Block Island's offshore wind farm often interferes with sonar used for communication, navigation, and echolocation by marine mammals that interferes with hearing and distorts their communication resulting in beaching, starvation and separation from the pod. Loud turbines can maim and kill fish by destroying their ability to self-regulate swim bladders necessary for their buoyancy in the water. Recently, forty-six whales, proven healthy by necropsy, were found beached in less than one year in this area. Forty-six of my friends. Gone. Healthy but confused. Now dead.

My reverie has lasted through the night. The sun peeks over the horizon, filling the sky with an orange glow. Soon, Cliff Walk would be filled with people. I feel the weight of the responsibility that rests with me. I am a highly intelligent, evolved being, capable of communication with both sea creatures and humans. The time to act is approaching. I return home to seek guidance from The Source—a luminous water hole over 100 feet below the surface—where pulsating energy ignites my body and clarifies my mind. I meditate, then pray for the fortitude needed to meet my destiny.

When the sun is at its highest point in the sky, the sounds of frantic clicking and whistling from Cliff Walk reverberate through the open water. The baby dolphin is in danger! It stuck its snout through one of the circles in the plastic six-pack rings, and now cannot open its mouth to eat or communicate. I rush back to Narragansett Bay. The terrified baby is swimming in circles, trying to evade the swimmers and boaters who have come to witness the calf's terrible plight. Help has arrived. Marine rescue units skillfully catch the calf in a net and bring it to the shallow area where the experienced team calms the dolphin while gently removing the deadly plastic. Upon being freed from the net, the calf bolts from the shoreline, following the sounds of its mother's cries. The crowd applauds, cameras capturing the spectacle.

Avalyn is standing at the shoreline. I must seize the moment. I swim to the shallow area, rise up, balancing on my monofin, and call to Avalyn to come closer. Only she can hear me.

"It is my wish to expand my language and telepathic skills so that I might effectively communicate my message to the land dwellers. Let me show you how humans, using the oceans to further your own ends, are altering and dismantling its balance."

Avalyn and I have a direct line of communication. Her face is radiant. She is transposed to another dimension. I silently convey my concerns, warnings, and solutions. Avalyn quickly absorbs the knowledge of the ages.

"I accept the challenge," she solemnly proclaims.

Whirling until a frothy maelstrom forms, suspended above the vortex by my newly discovered powers, I extend my arms toward the sky. I find my voice.

"I am Marina, Ruler of Merfolk."

Avalyn gasps as she hears my voice for the first time. The crowd murmurs in the background, afraid to intrude on this transformative moment.

"We exist in different realms, but we are one world. I name Avalyn as liaison between land and sea dwellers so we may cooperate for the good of all. Please heed her message. Our destinies depend on it."

RETURNING TO THE SEA

LINDA M. CRATE

Aruna had dreamed of the sea for as long as she had remembered. Her family warned her of the dangers of the deeps, but she could not stay away from the ocean. It was as if she recalled the loving embrace of the sea from lifetimes before or something. Her family didn't believe in past lives, but she did.

Aruna knew that just because someone didn't believe in something didn't mean that it wasn't in existence, it didn't happen, or it wasn't real.

Her family knew magic, but they didn't believe in past lives? Seemed fishy to her. How could they believe in so many things, but not believe in that? They said ignorance was bliss, but it wasn't for those who had to deal with the ignorance. She shook her head, gazing at the sea as she always did.

Aruna wondered if she would ever meet anyone who understood her or even tried to.

She was sick to death of being the strong one, the reliable one, the one that never broke or buckled beneath the pressure. She wanted to be vulnerable, authentic, to be able to feel her emotions without being judged. Aruna ran a hand through her wavy brown hair, laughing as moments later the winds picked up and decided to rearrange her hair completely.

Such was life, you intended on one thing and sometimes got something entirely different.

Yet Aruna had always wished she could've received a family who understood her instead of one that constantly found fault with her or her dreams because they didn't have the imagination to believe the possibility of impossible things.

They had always told her that patience was a virtue when she lost her patience with them, but how could she not? They always played it safe. Too safe. Without dreams, without risks, without the hope and roar of something new how could that be a promising life? Sure, they were safe but if nothing was ever ventured then nothing could be gained.

They always gave her grief about her temper, too, but they all had tempers of their own. Hers, at least, was slow burning but they claimed that was more dangerous because her temper could take out an entire forest.

Aruna thought that perhaps they ought not provoke her fury and her wrath then.

Could they not see her depths or her heights or the lands and seas between? Could they not see she wasn't always flowers and sunshine but also thorns and darkness? She hated their shallows, she required deeper waters in which to swim. Which is why Aruna thought she had always been drawn to the sea.

They always told her to be careful, but not once had she been attacked by any sea creature.

Aruna knew that they cared about her, but she thought they knew nothing about her if they thought she foolish enough to provoke any living creature within the sea. How long had she been dreaming, learning, and reading and experiencing the sea? Longer than she could honestly remember.

The day was dark and gloomy, but Aruna didn't care. She wanted to breathe in the salt water and feel the wind dance in her hair, and so she ran through the sand. She was a bit grateful for the dark cover because the sand wasn't burning her feet like it sometimes would on warmer days.

As soon as the sea kissed her feet, she felt as if she were in heaven.

She saw something moving in the water, and her heart dropped. Was it a shark? A jellyfish? A giant sea turtle? She had just gotten here, Aruna didn't want to leave already to her boring and average life where nothing exciting ever seemed to happen.

It was then that she realized it was none of these things, but rather a mermaid. She had read so many stories about mermaids, wondering if she would ever meet one; and here a mermaid was! Amazing! She didn't look entirely too friendly, though, so Aruna kept her distance. She couldn't help but be curious.

"Staring's rude, you know?" the mermaid said. "Is this your first time seeing a mermaid or something?"

Aruna nodded.

"Well, congratulations, you've seen me!" the mermaid said, sarcastically. She ran a hand through her long aquamarine hair, her green skin dotted with yellow and white freckles. "Do you have a name?"

"My name is Aruna," Aruna answered.

"They call me Marilee," the mermaid remarked. "Are you going to stop staring at me as if I am some kind of sea monster that wants to devour you?"

"I'm sorry," Aruna apologized, looking away. "I just didn't realize what a real mermaid would look like. They look different in our books than you. They don't have fangs or green skin."

"Humans are notorious for getting things wrong so I'm not surprised," Marilee responded. "What, do they think we eat seaweed instead of other fish, too?"

"Actually, some of them do say that," Aruna nodded.

Marilee rolled her eyes. "Of course they do," she muttered, shaking her head. "Kind of makes you wonder why my ancestors kept up the tradition of saving sailors," she murmured. "But I suppose making us seem nicer than we are would prevent someone from confusing a mermaid for a siren."

"Are sirens so similar that it's hard to know the difference?" Aruna frowned.

"Not really, I mean they all have allure, don't get me wrong; but you can see the evil in their eyes if you're really paying attention," Marilee remarked. "So it's easy to get away if you keep your wits about you. Unfortunately, some people see a pretty woman and fall straight in love...which makes them easy food for a siren."

"Aruna!"

Aruna turned to see her brother was calling her. He looked at the mermaid in horror.

"Aruna, get away from that thing before it kills you."

"It's a mermaid not a siren," Aruna argued, rolling her eyes. "Why are you even out here?" she asked, irritated. She would've loved to have more time to get to know this mermaid.

"Mother said it was time to get ready for lunch."

Aruna was hardly hungry at the moment so this only served to further annoy her. When she turned around Marilee was gone. Sighing, she shook her head, before grumpily hitching up her dress and stomping in the direction of her house.

Her family would ruin her first time meeting a mermaid. Of course they would! They had no imagination, and were all too content with their life outside of the sea. She didn't understand why they didn't love the ocean the way she did, could they not see the beauty of the ocean? Didn't they have any sense of wonder, at all? She couldn't imagine being so close to the ocean and never wanting to spend time in the water.

They caught fish, sold fish, served fish, ate fish.

She couldn't imagine doing that for the rest of her life. Aruna had always wanted something more than fish in her life. Knowing she could be talking to a mermaid instead of being bored to death at lunch further served to annoy her.

Wiping off her feet with a towel she walked upstairs to wash her hands before helping her mother finish setting up the table for lunch. When she sat down, her mother started hounding her.

"So, Aruna, have you even thought about getting married?" her mother asked her, her lips pursed.

Aruna coughed, slamming a fist into her chest. "Mother, I don't even have anyone? How would I be getting married without someone to marry?"

Her father laughed. "Besides, she's welcome to live with us as long as she wants. I don't want some stupid boy coming to take my daughter away," he said, winking at Aruna.

"At this rate Aruna's going to die alone," her brother crowed, looking amused.

Aruna rolled her eyes, sticking her tongue out at her brother.

"Aruna, that's not ladylike!" her mother scolded.

"Who said I was trying to be a lady? Maybe I was just trying to be me," Aruna shrugged. Besides she was only twenty, who said she was going to die alone? Maybe she would marry, maybe she never would. Who knew, who cared? She would live her life as she wished. She wished her mother would stop wheedling her about a wedding.

"All of your other sisters were married at eighteen or nineteen," her mother continued.

"I know, mama," Aruna remarked. She was a little tired of hearing about her sisters and how they were married off at a young age. Didn't her mother understand that she was interested in following her own heart, not whatever mumbo jumbo that society insisted and deemed respectable?

"Even your oldest brother finally left home and got married and he's so happy," her mother insisted.

"I know, mama."

"Why can't you be more like your sisters?" her mother demanded.

"Because I am me, mama!" Aruna shouted. "I'm sorry I'm not perfect like my sisters," she scowled, leaping to her feet. She stormed out of the house, slamming the door behind her.

She heard her mother, father, and brother all calling for her; but she ignored them all. Aruna couldn't understand why her mother had to nag so much, why her father never intervened, or why her brother had to egg on her mother.

She stepped towards the water, feeling tranquility when the sea rushed in to meet her. Ah yes, this was bliss.

"Back again, are you?" Marilee asked. "What's eating you?" she asked, taking one look at Aruna's face.

"My family won't leave me alone. They poke and they prod and they expect me to be a certain way, but I am someone else entirely,"

Aruna answered. "My mother keeps trying to push me into marriage, insists all my other sisters were married off at eighteen or nineteen so I should already be married. She doesn't take into account that only three of those six marriages are happy, and I don't like those odds. I just want to be happy, I just want a chance to be me. I am so sick of being strong, reliable, and the one that always does what is expected of her. Why should I hold my tongue and allow myself to be miserable forever just because it would make them happy?!"

"What does your father say?"

"He says nothing, just lets her go on and on and on," Aruna scowled. "I just wish he would tell her off, just once. Maybe he agrees that I should be married, I don't know. My brother just eggs her on, thinks it's hilarious when I get upset. None of them even understand or know who I am. They only care about how the family appears to others. They don't care about me."

Marilee frowned. "That's rough. I'm sorry, Aruna," she responded. "Maybe they just don't understand how they make you feel."

"I've told them before, but they refuse to listen. They'll say I'm being ungrateful or that I ask for too much or that I need to get my head out of the clouds and let go of my dreams. They say the impossible never happens as if impossible things don't happen every day. I just want to be free of them, to experience the sea again. I think I must've been here in a past life because I love the sea. Don't ask me as what or who, I don't know. All I know is that I am so sick of suffering," Aruna told Marilee, feeling tears course down her cheeks.

Marilee frowned. "Well, let me talk to my father, but maybe we can do something to help. Stay here, okay? I'll be back in a the flick of a fish fin."

Aruna couldn't help but offer her a small smile. "Okay," she responded.

She watched as Marilee leapt in and out of the sea until she was out of sight. She meant what she had said, though. She was sick of swallowing herself down for the sake of others who didn't even try to understand who she was.

Aruna just wished there was a way out. An escape she could take.

Marilee came back an hour later, holding what looked to be a potion in her hands. "I have a proposition for you," she said. "Father says you can be a mermaid and join us in the sea. But there's a catch. If you come to the sea, then you cannot return back to land again."

Aruna thought of her mother and father. They loved her, but they didn't love her in the way she needed to be loved. She thought of her brothers and her sisters. She knew that she would never see them again, and it made her feel conflicted. Yet there was another part of her that said an adventure like this wouldn't ever be promised to her again.

"You don't have to take the potion," Marilee remarked. "Don't feel guilty on my behalf."

"I know that I'll miss them," Aruna began. "But I also know if I stay that things won't get any better," she remarked. The wind danced through her hair. "They're not bad people, they just don't understand me and I don't think that's going to change." She looked at Marilee. "I'm willing to leave this all behind me."

"Are you sure? There's no changing your mind once you come into the waters as one of us," Marilee warned her.

"I'm ready," Aruna nodded.

"Then take this. Father said it might not taste great, but it will transform you into one of us."

Aruna nodded at Marilee's words, uncorking the bottle. As she drank it, she had to agree that it didn't taste good. But after she had finished the bottle, she gasped in surprise. Her skin was not green like Marilee's but carnelian and gold like a sunset, and her red tail was such a beautiful shade of crimson. "I look like a sunset," Aruna remarked, running a hand through her hair; which she noticed was still brown.

"You do," Marilee agreed.

Aruna laughed, trying out her fins in the water; her heart soaring. Yes, she thought to herself, she was making the right decision. She was a mermaid returning to the sea!

"What will your family think?"

"That I got pulled out to sea, probably," Aruna shrugged. "But it's okay, they can think whatever helps them deal with the loss of me. I know this is where I am meant to be."

Aruna didn't care if it was selfish, if it was cruel, or if it were wrong to leave her family. Her entire life she had spent her life trying to please and help and be there for others. She was going to live her life now for her. She was going to follow her own heart, life was too short to be unhappy with it.

In the end she had to do what was best for herself no matter who it might offend.

Aruna knew that being here with Marilee was in her best interest. "Can I meet your family or your friends?" she asked.

"Of course," Marilee nodded. "Let's get going then?"

Aruna nodded, giggling as she joined Marilee in leaping in and out of the sea until they dove into the depths of the water where no human could follow. She felt excitement in her veins as she followed Marilee. Her family would never understand, but she knew she was where she was meant to be. She was living the adventure she had always wanted, and she knew she would never regret this.

ABOUT THE AUTHORS

SUZANNE BAGINSKIE

Suzanne Baginskie retired from a twenty-nine-year career as an office manager/paralegal in a law office. She's sold several short mysteries, romance stories and over twenty non-fiction stories to Chicken Soup for the Soul books and Cup of Comfort. Her first published book came out October, 2021, by Magnolia Blossom Publishing. Dangerous Charade is Book One in her FBI Affairs series, Book Two, Dangerous Revenge is out now. Her short stories appear in Red Penguin's Behind Closed Doors Anthology, A Heart Full of Love Collection, Woman's World, Plan B Mystery Magazine, The Wrong Side of the Law, two Daily Flash Fiction volumes, Woman's World Magazine, First Magazine, True Romance Magazine, Guideposts, Futures Magazine and Turbulence & Coffee. She is a member of MWA, FMWA and Sisters-in-Crime and The Short Mystery Fiction Society. Her website is: www.suzannebaginskie.webador.com

LINDA M. CRATE

Linda M. Crate (she/her) is a Pennsylvanian writer whose poetry, short stories, articles, and reviews have been published in a myriad of magazines both online and in print. She has eleven published chapbooks: A Mermaid Crashing Into Dawn (Fowlpox Press - June 2013), Less Than A Man (The Camel Saloon - January 2014), If Tomorrow Never Comes (Scars Publications, August 2016), My Wings Were Made to Fly (Flutter Press, September 2017), splintered with terror (Scars Publications, January 2018), More Than Bone Music (Clare Songbirds

Publishing House, March 2019), the samurai (Yellow Arrowing Publishing, October 2020), Follow the Black Raven (Alien Buddha Publishing, July 2021), Unleashing the Archers (Guerilla Genesis Press, August 2021), Hecate's Child (Alien Buddha Publishing, November 2021) and fat & pretty (Dancing Girl Press, June 2022), and three micro-chapbooks Heaven Instead (Origami Poems Project, May 2018), moon mother (Origami Poems Project, March 2020), and & so I believe (Origami Poems Project, April 2021). She is also the author of the novella Mates (Alien Buddha Publishing, March 2022).

ELAINE DONADIO

Author. Poet. Blogger. Book reviewer. Former Reading Specialist at New York City Schools, Elaine Donadio's characters reflect the urban lifestyle. She writes about what she loves, using well-researched facts to feed your head, your heart, and your soul. She's concerned about the effects of human carelessness on the world in which we live. Learning is the point but better viewed through experiences that communicate awe as the world unfolds its secrets. Readers can laugh and learn at the same time.

Study guides in alignment with state standards for science, social studies, and literacy are available at elainedonadio.com.

R. J. ERBACHER

I was walking on the beach one night in Aruba about twenty years ago and as I looked out over the sea, I saw a storm that was so far away I could see the lightning strikes but couldn't hear the thunder. I wondered about the emotions coursing through someone who was trapped in a storm like that. How scary would that be? Then I thought, what if you didn't even have a boat, if you were just being tossed about on the waves by the ocean. What a helpless situation but more importantly, why were you out there? The majority of this story came to me in a flash and I went back to my room and wrote until sunrise, starring out the balcony doors to the black sea for inspiration. I've never had a story develop that quickly before or since. "Love of the Black Lady" was truly a tale inspired by the sea. I do hope you enjoyed it.

SHARI HELD

Shari Held is an Indianapolis-based, award-winning fiction author who spins tales of romance, horror, fantasy, and mystery. Her short stories have been published in numerous magazines and anthologies, including Hoosier Noir, Homicide for the Holidays, Asinine Assassins, and Murder 20/20, for which she served as co-editor. Her short stories have appeared in several Red Penguin Collection anthologies, including Between the Covers, Pets on the Prowl, and The Dating Game. When not writing, she cares for feral cats and other wildlife, reads, and strategizes imaginative ways for characters and trouble to collide!

DAVID LANGE

David Lange was born and grew up on Long Island, New York. A graduate of the United States Air Force Academy, he served for 30 years as an Active Duty officer in the United States Air Force before retiring in 2018. Colonel Lange is a decorated combat veteran and flew numerous combat, combat support, and humanitarian relief missions during his career. He was awarded the prestigious Institute of Navigation Superior Achievement Award in recognition of his life-long accomplishments as a practicing navigator. David loves sharing stories of hope and inspiration. He has numerous short stories, essays, and poems published within various anthologies and his memoir, "Quest: My Journey Through La Mancha," was published in 2020.

PAUL MILA

Paul Mila has expanded his horizons from Brooklyn to Baja and beyond. He traded in his corporate suit for a wetsuit and now devotes his time to writing, scuba diving, underwater photography, and speaking to groups, especially children, about ocean conservation and protecting sea turtles.

He has enjoyed photographing and diving with Caribbean reef sharks in the Bahamas, humpback whales in the Dominican Republic and Tonga, great white sharks at Guadalupe Island, Mexico, sea turtles in Cozumel, Mexico, and a wide variety of sea life around the world, including his home waters of Long Island, New York.

Recently he has written the children's books Harry Hawksbill Helps His Friends, Gracie Green Turtle Finds her Beach, and Larry Loggerhead Travels to the Sea Turtle Hospital, published by Best Publishing Company. These books feature Paul's underwater photography of sea turtles and other marine life, while telling educational and fun stories.

He is also the author of six underwater thrillers, the Manetta Mystery Adventure Series, and has co-authored Bubbles Up, a non-fiction collection of ocean adventures and sea-creature encounters.

Visit his website: www.milabooks.com

MICHAEL O'KEEFE

Michael O'Keefe is a retired 1st Grade Detective from the NYPD, a novelist, poet, and playwright, and the author of the acclaimed Detective Paddy Durr Series. O'Keefe likes retirement, but he loved homicide investigation and would still be doing it if he hadn't been injured in the line of duty and disabled. He lives on Long Island with his family, where he coaches football and writes.

WILLIAM JOHN ROSTRON

William John Rostron is the author of a series of novels steeped in the late 20th and early 21st centuries' music and culture. Band in the Wind, Sound of Redemption, and Brotherhood of Forever have received critical acclaim from Writers Digest, the Online Book Club Review, and many other reviewers. These books have found readership on four continents (North America, Europe, Australia, and Asia). He has been published in seventeen Red Penguin anthologies and four Visible Ink anthologies. The Visible Ink pieces have been produced for the New York stage and are available for viewing on the author's website. www.WilliamJohnRostron.com. An anthology of short pieces entitled A Flamingo Under the Carousel has recently been published by Red Penguin Books.

Born and raised in Queens, NY, William John Rostron now splits his time between his home on Eastern Long Island and traveling the country in his Tiffin motorhome. When not writing, he is busy completing a bucket list of travel adventures. In the past 17 years, he and his wife Marilyn have traveled 140,000 miles. These journeys have taken them to the 48 contiguous states, 133 national parks, all 30 major league baseball stadiums, 154 cities and towns, two Canadian provinces, and a variety of unusual experiences and locations. Many of these locations have served as backgrounds for his books.

He presently working on a fourth novel entitled Lost in the Wind and a second book of short stories.

www.WilliamJohnRostron.com

JASMINE TRITTEN

Jasmine Tritten is an award-winning author born in Denmark. In 1964 she immigrated to the U.S.A. The last five years she has written numerous short stories published in various anthologies. Her memoir The Journey of an Adventuresome Dane, published in 2015, won an award. A children's story, Kato's Grand Adventure, published in 2018, she wrote with her husband. It won five awards. During the pandemic in 2020, Jasmine wrote and self-published a travel book On the Nile with a Dancing Dane which won three awards in 2021. Jasmine resides in enchanting Corrales, New Mexico with her husband and four cats.

JIM TRITTEN

Jim Tritten is a retired Navy carrier pilot who now lives in a semi-rural village in New Mexico with his Danish author/artist wife and four cats.

ALSO FROM THE RED PENGUIN COLLECTION

FICTION

What Lies Beyond – Sci-Fi Stories of the Future

I Can't Find My Flashlight – Contemporary Campfire Stories

A Heart Full of Love – A Collection of Romantic Short Stories

Behind Closed Doors – A Mystery Anthology

Once Upon A Time… – A Fairy Tale Anthology

Ernest Lived …and other Historical Fiction Short Stories

Until Dawn – A Supernatural Anthology

Treat-or-Trick – Halloween Horror Stories

Pets On the Prowl – An Animal Mystery Anthology

My Robot & Me – A Not-So Fiction Anthology

POETRY

Words for the Earth – A Poetry Project

'Tis The Seasons – Poems to Lift Your Holiday Spirits

the flower shop on the corner – A Spring Poetry Anthology

the ocean waves – A Summer Poetry Anthology

the leaves fall – An Autumnal Poetry Anthology

Proud to Be – A Pride Poetry Collection

THE STAND OUT SERIES

Stand Out – The Best of The Red Penguin Collection, Vol. 1

Stand Out – The Best of The Red Penguin Collection, Vol. 2

www.ingramcontent.com/pod-product-compliance
Lightning Source LLC
Chambersburg PA
CBHW050450110726
47899CB00003B/885